BLESSED ARE THOSE WHO THIRST

This Large Print Book carries the
Seal of Approval of N.A.V.H.

A HANNE WILHELMSEN NOVEL

BLESSED ARE THOSE WHO THIRST

ANNE HOLT

Translated from the Norwegian by Anne Bruce

THORNDIKE PRESS
A part of Gale, Cengage Learning

GALE
CENGAGE Learning·

Detroit • New York • San Francisco • New Haven, Conn • Waterville, Maine • London

GALE
CENGAGE Learning®

LIBRARY OF CONGRESS CATALOGING-IN-PUBLICATION DATA

Holt, Anne, 1958–
  [Salige er de som Tørster. English]
  Blessed are those who thirst : a Hanne Wilhelmsen novel / by Anne Holt ; translated from the Norwegian by Anne Bruce. — Large Print edition.
    pages cm. — (Thorndike Press Large Print Thriller)
  "Originally published in Norwegian as Salige er de som Tørster"—T.p. verso.
  ISBN 978-1-4104-5898-8 (hardcover) — ISBN 1-4104-5898-9 (hardcover)
  1. Large type books. I. Title.
  PT8952.18.O386B5413 2013
  839.82'374—dc23   2013007321

Published in 2013 by arrangement with Scribner, a division of Simon & Schuster, Inc.

Printed in the United States of America
1 2 3 4 5 6 7 17 16 15 14 13

To Even, my friend and brother

Blessed are those who hunger and thirst after righteousness, for they will be filled.

— MATTHEW 5:6

SUNDAY, MAY 9

It was so early not even the devil had managed to put on his shoes. In the west, the heavens showed that intense hue only a Scandinavian sky in springtime is blessed with — royal blue on the horizon and lighter toward the meridian, before dissolving into a pink eiderdown where the sun was still lying lazily in the east. The air was invigorating, undisturbed by the dawn, with that amazing transparency possessed by radiant spring mornings at almost sixty degrees north. Although the temperature remained in single figures, everything indicated it would be another warm May day in Oslo.

Detective Inspector Hanne Wilhelmsen wasn't thinking about the weather. She was standing completely motionless, wondering what she should do. There was blood everywhere. On the floor. Across the walls. Even on the ceiling, dark spatters resembled the abstract pictures in some kind of psychological test. She tilted her head and stared at a splodge directly above her. It looked like a purple bull with three horns and deformed hindquarters. She stood motionless — a sign of indecision, but also an indication of her fear of sliding on the slippery floor.

"Don't touch," she warned brusquely, when a younger colleague, who had hair color to match the blood, made a move to lay his finger on one of the walls. A narrow crack in the ramshackle roof cast a dusty beam of light on the rear wall, where the blood was spread so generously it looked less like a drawing than a horrendously bad paint job.

"Go outside," she ordered. Hanne sighed but refrained from commenting on the footprints the inexperienced police constable had scattered around large areas of the floor. "And try to walk in your own footprints on your way out."

A couple of minutes later, she did the same herself, backward and hesitant. She continued to stand in the doorway, having sent the officer for a flashlight.

"I was just going for a piss," wheezed the man who had called in the report. Obediently, he had remained standing outside the shed. Now he was hopping so agitatedly Hanne Wilhelmsen suspected he hadn't been able to complete his mission an hour earlier.

"The lavatory is there," he said, quite unnecessarily. The strong smell from one of Oslo's all too many remaining outside toilets took the edge off the sickeningly sweet stench of blood. The door marked with a heart was right beside it.

"Well, off you go to the toilet," she encouraged him in a friendly tone, but he didn't hear her.

"I was going for a piss, you see, but then I saw the door in there was open."

Now he pointed at the woodshed, taking a step backward, as though a hideous animal might thrust out its jaws at any moment and gobble up his whole arm.

"It's usually closed. Not actually locked, but closed. The door is so heavy it stays open by itself. We don't want stray dogs and cats making themselves at home in there. So we're quite careful about that."

A strange little smile spread across his coarse face. It occurred to Hanne that they looked after things even in this neighborhood; they had rules and kept order, even though the battle against decay was being lost.

"I've lived here in this block all my life," he continued, with a touch of pride. "I

11

notice when things aren't as they should be."

He glanced at the pretty young lady who didn't look like any cop he had seen before, waiting for a scrap of recognition.

"Good stuff," she praised him. "It was great you phoned to let us know."

When he smiled, with his mouth open, Hanne was struck by how few teeth he possessed. He couldn't be very old, perhaps fifty.

"I was absolutely terrified, you understand. All that blood . . ."

His head moved from side to side. It had been awful, being faced with such a diabolical sight.

Hanne could well appreciate that. Her red-haired colleague had returned with a flashlight. Gripping it with both hands, Hanne Wilhelmsen shone the beam of light systematically from side to side down over the walls. She scrutinized the ceiling as thoroughly as was possible from the doorway, and then zigzagged the ray of light across the floor.

The room was entirely empty. Not so much as a stick of firewood, only some odds and ends attesting that the shed had once been used for its original purpose, probably a long time ago. Once the flashlight had made contact with every single square meter, she ventured into the shed once more, carefully stepping on her own old footprints. She gave a hand signal that told her colleague not to follow. Right in the middle of the room, approximately fifteen square meters, she hunkered down. The beam of light stirred on the wall opposite, about a meter above the floor. From the doorway she had noticed something, perhaps letters, written in smeared blood, making the symbols difficult to decipher.

They weren't letters. They were numbers. Eight digits, as far as she could make out: 92043576. The figure 9 was unclear and might perhaps be 4. The final digit looked like a 6, but she was not sure. Maybe it was an 8 instead. She straightened up and stepped back again into the daylight, now abundant. She heard a baby crying from an open window on the second floor and shuddered at the thought of children having to live in such a district. A Pakistani in a tram driver's uniform emerged from the brick building, peering nosily at them for a moment before scurrying away from the entrance. She could see in the reflections on the highest windows that the sun had hauled itself up at last. Birds, the small gray ones that still managed to eke out a meager existence in the innermost center of the city, were chirping tentatively from a half-dead birch tree that was making a futile attempt to reach out toward the streaks of morning light.

"Bloody hell, what a terrible crime this must be," the young constable commented as he spat, in a vain effort at ridding himself of the taste of sewage. "Something terrible must have happened here!"

He seemed happy at the thought.

"Yes indeed," Hanne Wilhelmsen said softly. "Something serious may well have happened here. But in the meantime . . ."

She broke off and turned to face her colleague.

"At the moment, this isn't a crime. For that, we need a victim. We haven't seen a single trace of that. At the most, this is willful vandalism. But . . ."

She peered through the door again.

"Of course, something might turn up. Contact Forensics. It's best to be on the safe side."

She shivered slightly. It was due more to her speculation about what she had just witnessed rather than the fresh morning air. Pulling her jacket snugly around her, she thanked the toothless man one more time for alerting them before strolling on her own

14

back the three hundred meters to Oslo police headquarters. When she crossed over to the other side of the street, into range of the morning sunlight, it grew warmer. A tumult of international women's voices, morning shouts in Urdu, Punjabi, and Arabic, reverberated around the corners of the houses. A kiosk owner was going about his business, readying his sidewalk stand for another long working day, opening out the whole shebang with no consideration for either churchgoing or regulations about opening hours. He flashed a friendly white smile at her, holding out an orange and raising his eyebrows questioningly. Hanne Wilhelmsen shook her head and smiled in return. A gang of fourteen-year-old boys was clattering over the sidewalk with their blue *Aftenposten* newspaper delivery buggies in tow. Two veiled women hurried to some destination or other, eyes downcast. They walked in a large arc around the detective inspector, unused to seeing white women so early in the day. Otherwise, it was fairly deserted. In this weather, even Tøyen took on a conciliatory, almost charming character.

It certainly promised to be yet another beautiful day.

Monday, May 10

"What on earth were you working on over the weekend? Don't you think we have enough of a slog every day of the week?"

Police Attorney Håkon Sand was standing in the doorway. His jeans were new, and for once he was wearing a jacket and tie. His jacket was slightly too large and his tie was a touch too broad, but nevertheless he looked reasonably put together. Apart from the hemline on his jeans. Hanne Wilhelmsen couldn't resist leaning in front of him, speedily tucking the superfluous centimeters inside so they couldn't be seen.

"You shouldn't walk about with the turn-up on the outside." She gave a friendly smile and stood up. She smoothed her hand down his arm with a light, almost tender, movement.

"There. Now you're fantastic. Are you going to court?"

"No," replied the prosecution attorney,

who, despite the well-meaning gesture, felt embarrassed. Why did the detective inspector have to draw attention to his lack of fashion sense? She could have saved herself the trouble of doing that, he thought, though he said something different.

"I've a dinner date right after work. But what about you, why were you here?"

A pale green folder hung poised in the air before landing precisely on Hanne Wilhelmsen's blotter.

"I just received this," he went on. "Strange case. There have been no reports of either dismembered people or animals in our area."

"I did an extra shift in the crime section," she explained, leaving the folder untouched. "They're struggling with illness down there right now."

The police prosecution attorney, a dark-haired and reasonably good-looking man whose temples were grayer than his thirty-five years would suggest, flopped onto the visitor's chair. He removed his glasses and sat polishing them with the end of his tie. The spectacles did not become particularly clean, but the tie became decidedly more crumpled.

"The case has been assigned to the two of us. If there is a case, that is. There's no victim, no one has heard anything, no one has seen anything. Odd. There are some pictures in there."

He pointed toward the folder.

"I don't need those, thanks." She waved dismissively. "I was there. It really didn't look very pretty.

"But you know," she continued, leaning toward him, "if all of that turns out to be human blood, then there must have been two or three people killed in there. I'm inclined to think there are some young hooligans having some fun with us."

The theory didn't seem improbable. The Oslo police were in the middle of their worst spring ever. In the course of six weeks, three murders had been visited upon the city, and at least one of these seemed unsolvable. There had been no fewer than sixteen cases of rape reported in the same period, with seven of these becoming the object of enormous media attention. The fact that one of the victims was a member of Parliament for the Christian Democrats, on her way home from an evening committee meeting when she was brutally assaulted in the Palace Park, inflamed public disappointment in the lack of progress made by the police. Well aided by the tabloid press, the frustrated citizens of Oslo had started to protest against the Oslo police's apparent inability to act. The elongated, curved building sat there at Grønlandsleiret 44, gray and unshakable, seemingly unmoved by all the merciless criticism. Its inhabitants arrived at work in the mornings with shoulders drawn up and eyes downcast. They went home again far too late each day, their backs bent and nothing more to show for their daily toil than still more confirmed dead ends. The weather gods played around tauntingly with intense summer temperatures. The awnings were pulled right down, in vain, over all the windows on the south façade of the enormous building, making it appear both blind and deaf. The interior remained just as stifling. Nothing helped, and nothing seemed to show the way out of a professional blind alley that simply increased with every new case entered into the huge data systems. They should be of assistance but instead appeared hostile, almost mocking, each morning when they spewed out their lists of unsolved cases.

"What a springtime," Hanne Wilhelmsen said, sighing theatrically. With a look of resignation, she raised her eyebrows and contemplated her superior officer. Her eyes were not especially large, but they were amazingly blue, with a distinctive black edge around the iris making them appear darker than they were. Her hair was dark brown and quite short. From time to time she tugged at it absentmindedly, as though she actually wished it were long and thought it would hasten its growth if she helped it along a little. Her mouth was generous, with a cupid's bow that didn't simply dip down from the top but also met its twin from below, like a hesitant cleft lip that had changed its mind, thus forming a sensuous curve instead of a defect. Above her left eye she bore a scar parallel to her eyebrow. It was pale pink and not particularly old.

"I've never seen it like this. Though I've only been here for eleven years. Kaldbakken has been here for thirty. He hasn't experienced anything like it, either."

She pulled at her T-shirt and gave it a shake.

"And this heat doesn't make it any better. The whole city is on the move every single night. A spell of rain right now would be just the thing. That would at least keep people indoors."

They sat there for too long, talking about everything and nothing. They were friendly colleagues who always had something to talk about but who didn't know very much about each other all the same. Other than that they both enjoyed their work, that they took it seriously, and that one of them was more competent than the other. That didn't do much for the relationship between them. She was a highly skilled officer with a reputation that had always been good but following a dramatic case the previous autumn had now reached legendary heights. He had loafed around in the police station as a second-rate lawyer for more than six years, never outstanding, never brilliant. Still, he had built up a reputation for himself as both conscientious and hardworking. He too had played a decisive role in the same sensational case. His reputation was edging more in the direction of solid and dependable than what it had been before: rather uninteresting.

Perhaps they complemented each other. Perhaps it was more the fact they were never in competition that enabled them to work so well together. However, it was a curious friendship, restricted by the walls of the police station. Police Attorney Håkon Sand was genuinely sorry about that and several times had endeavored to alter the situation. Some time ago he had suggested in passing that they meet up for dinner. The rejection had been so blunt it would be a long time before he made the effort again.

"Oh, well, we'll let the blood-soaked woodshed lie. I've got other things to do."

The police officer slapped a heap of files sitting in a tray beside the window.

"So have we all," the attorney retorted, before walking the twenty meters along the corridor to return to his own office.

"Why have you never brought me here before?"

The woman sitting on the opposite side of the narrow table smiled reproachfully as she squeezed her companion's hand.

"I didn't really know whether you liked this type of food," the man responded, clearly pleased at how successful the meal had been.

The Pakistani waiters, immaculately dressed and with diction indicating they had been born at Aker Hospital rather than a delivery room in Karachi, had amiably steered them through the menu.

"Slightly inconvenient location," he added. "But otherwise it's one of my favorite restaurants. Good food, top-notch service, and prices to suit a public servant."

"So you've been here often." She paused. "Who with, then?"

He didn't answer but instead raised his glass to hide how mortified he was by the question. All his women had been here. The very short-lived, far fewer than he liked to consider, and the two or three he had endured for a few months. Every time he had been thinking of her. What it would be like to sit here with Karen Borg. And now they were sitting here.

"Don't think about the ones who were first. Concentrate on being last," he said with a grin after a moment's thought.

"Elegantly put," she replied, but her voice had adopted a trace of . . . not coldness, but a kind of coolness that always terrified him out of his wits. That he could never learn.

Karen Borg didn't want to talk about the future. For almost four months she had been meeting him regularly, up to several times a week. They ate together and went to the theater. They went for walks in the forest, and they made love as soon as they had the opportunity. Which was not too often. She was married, so her apartment was out of the question. Her husband knew they were having an affair, she said, but they had decided not to burn their bridges until they were certain that was what they wanted. Of course they could go to his place, something he suggested every time they were together. But she turned him down flat.

"If I come home with you, then I've made a choice," she declared illogically.

Håkon Sand believed the choice of making love with him was a far more dramatic decision than the choice of venue, but it was no use. The waiter appeared with the check twenty seconds after Håkon had dropped a hint. It was presented according to old-fashioned etiquette, neatly folded on a plate placed in front of him. Karen Borg grabbed it, and he couldn't muster the energy to protest. It was one thing that she earned five times as much as he did and quite another to be continually reminded of that. When the AmEx gold card was returned, he got up and held her chair for her. The strikingly handsome waiter had ordered a taxicab, and she snuggled up to her lover in the backseat.

"I suppose you're going straight home," he said, a precaution against his own disappointment.

"Yes, it's a working day tomorrow," she confirmed. "We'll meet up again soon. I'll phone you."

Once she was out the taxi door, she leaned back in again to give him a gentle kiss.

"Thanks for a lovely evening," she said softly, smiling briefly as she withdrew from the cab once again.

24

Sighing, he gave the taxi driver a new address. It was situated in a completely different part of the city, allowing plenty of time to feel the sharp little stab of pain he always experienced after his evenings with Karen Borg.

SUNDAY, MAY 16

"Well, that's absolutely amazing."

Håkon Sand and Hanne Wilhelmsen were in agreement after all. It was quite strange.

Rain was drizzling. It was welcome after the completely abnormal tropical heat of the past few weeks. The garage was of the open type, one story supporting another on pillars with several meters' space between. No wall separated the weather from the few cars left behind in the cheerless building. Nonetheless, it didn't seem that any of the blood had washed away.

"Nothing else? No weapon or anything? No young girl missing?"

It was the police prosecution attorney speaking. Håkon was wearing a jogging suit and Helly Hansen jacket, and yawning despite the violent scene around him. Blood was spattered across one corner on the first floor of the parking lot. He knew from bitter experience that blood had an ugly tendency to spread widely, but what he saw here had to have taken many liters.

"Good that you phoned," he said, smothering a fresh yawn and glancing discreetly at his Swatch. It was half past five on Sunday morning. A car filled with celebrating students tore past, leaving the deafening blasts of a horn concerto in its wake. Then it was as quiet again as it always was after all the night owls had gone home to bed, safe in the knowledge no one needed an early rise.

"Yes, you had to see this. Fortunately there was a good pal of mine on duty, and she remembered I was involved in the first of these . . ."

Hanne Wilhelmsen didn't quite know what to call these absurd cases.

". . . these Saturday night massacres," she concluded, after a brief pause. "I got here half an hour ago."

The two men from Forensics were in full swing, taking samples and photographs. They worked quickly and with great precision, and neither of them uttered a word as they went about their business. Hanne and Håkon also remained silent for some considerable time. In the distance, the car full of students had encountered acquaintances, and the jangle of their horn broke the

27

silence once again.

"This has to mean something. Look at that!"

Håkon Sand made an attempt to follow a straight line from the point of her finger toward the wall. The light was poor, but the numbers were outlined clearly enough once his attention was drawn to them.

"Nine-two-six-four-seven-eight-three-five," he read aloud. "Does that mean anything to you?"

"Absolutely nothing. Other than it being the same number of digits as the last time, and the first two are the same."

"Couldn't it be a telephone number?"

"That area code doesn't exist. I've considered that, of course."

"National Insurance number?"

She didn't answer.

"Of course not," he brushed it aside himself. "There's no such month as the ninetieth . . ."

"Besides, there's either two digits too many or three too few."

"But abroad, the date of birth is the other way around," Håkon Sand recalled enthusiastically. "They begin with the year!"

"Right, well. Then we have a murderer who was born on the seventy-eighth day of the sixty-fourth month in 1992."

28

An uncomfortable silence ensued, but Hanne Wilhelmsen was kindhearted enough not to let it last too long.

"The blood is being analyzed. Also, there must be fingerprints here somewhere. We'd better go home. I hope it was okay for me to phone. See you tomorrow."

"Tomorrow? But it's the seventeenth!"

"Bloody hell, right enough," she said, stifling a yawn. "Personally, I boycott that day, but I don't mind having a day off."

"Boycott the seventeenth of May?" He was genuinely shocked.

"A day for regional costumes, flags, and other nationalistic nonsense. I prefer to plant up my window box."

He didn't quite know whether she was being serious. If this was true, she had told him something about herself for the very first time. That fact meant he was on cloud nine all the way home. Even though he himself adored the 17th of May.

TUESDAY, MAY 18

Norway's National Day had been one of the good old kind. The sun had poured its warmth over the country and the bright green trees of springtime. The royal family stood steadfastly waving from their vast balcony. Tired, sullen children in mini–folk costumes with ice cream splashes trailed their little flags along the ground, despite the encouraging cheers of overeager parents. Hoarse, drunken students devastated everything in sight as though it were their last day on earth and their intention was to achieve the highest possible blood alcohol count on the road to the hereafter. The Norwegian people enjoyed themselves with their Constitution and lashings of eggnog, and everyone was in total agreement it had been a marvelous day.

Apart from the Oslo police. They saw everything most of the others were fortunate to avoid. Disorderly conduct, overintoxicated citizens, unruly teenagers, one or two drunk drivers, and a few instances of domestic disturbance: all of this was to be expected and so could be handled with ease. A brutal murder and five other stabbing assaults were above and beyond the norm. To top it all off, there were five new cases of rape. That year's 17th of May would enter history as the toughest ever.

"I can't understand what's happening in this city. I just can't fathom it."

Chief Inspector Kaldbakken, in charge of A 2.11, Homicide Division, at Oslo police headquarters, had served longer than any of the others in the room. He was a man of few words, and those he uttered were usually incomprehensible mumbles. But this time they all understood.

"I've never experienced anything like it."

The others stared into space, and no one said anything. They were all painfully aware of what the crime wave would mean.

"Overtime," one of the male officers eventually muttered, his gaze fixed grimly on a wall collage, pictures from the previous year's summer party. "Overtime, overtime. The wife's as grouchy as an old crab."

"Are there still funds in the overtime budget?" asked a young female officer with short blonde hair and vestiges of an optimistic view on life.

She didn't receive an immediate answer, only a reproachful look from the superintendent that told the more experienced ones in the room what they all knew already.

"Sorry, folks, but if this continues, then holidays will have to be postponed," he said.

Three of the eleven police officers present in the conference room had booked their vacations for August and September, and now they sent up a silent prayer of thanks for their own foresight. By that time it would probably have calmed down.

They divided the tasks as well as they could. There was not even any attempt to pay attention to how their previous caseloads looked. They were all in a similarly difficult position.

Hanne Wilhelmsen was spared the murder. To compensate, she was allocated two of the rape cases as well as three assaults. Erik Henriksen, the police constable with the ginger hair, would assist her. He appeared happy at the thought. Hanne gave a deep sigh, rising to her feet when the cases were distributed and wondering all the way back to her office where on earth she should start.

SATURDAY, MAY 22

The evening hadn't advanced further than the Saturday TV documentary before Hanne Wilhelmsen nodded off. Her live-in partner, a woman of the same age, their birthdays only three weeks apart, hadn't glimpsed her all week long. Even on Ascension Thursday, a public holiday, Hanne had disappeared at daybreak, returning home around nine o'clock to collapse into bed. Today they had made up for lost time. They slept late, rode the motorbike for four hours, and stopped at roadside cafés to eat ice cream. They felt like sweethearts for the first time in ages. Although Hanne had slept through a cheesy Saturday matinee while Cecilie prepared dinner, she had hardly finished devouring the food, and at most half a bottle of red wine, when she flaked out on the settee. Cecilie wasn't sure whether she should be annoyed or flattered. Deciding on the latter, she spread a blanket over her partner and whispered in her ear, "You must be really sure of me, you know."

The sweet scent of female skin and faint perfume kept her there. She kissed her gently on the cheek, letting the tip of her tongue move light as a feather across the fine hairs on the sleeping woman's cheek as she made up her mind to wake her after all.

An hour and a half later, the phone rang. It was Hanne's phone. They could tell by the tone. Cecilie's phone had a ringing sound, Hanne's a chime. That they had two telephones with separate numbers wounded Cecilie deeply. Hanne's phone was never to be touched by anyone but herself, as no one from Oslo police headquarters was to know she shared a house with another woman. The phone system was one of the few incontestable rules on which their fifteen-year-long live-in partnership was founded.

It didn't stop. If it had been Cecilie's phone, they would have let it ring until it gave up. All the same, its insistent sound indicated it might be something important. Groaning, Hanne hauled herself up to stand naked in the doorway leading to the hallway, with her back to the bedroom.

"Wilhelmsen, go ahead!"

"Iversen, on duty, here. Sorry to phone so late . . ."

Hanne glanced at the clock on the kitchen wall, just visible from where she was standing. Well past midnight.

"No, it's perfectly all right." She yawned, shivering slightly in the faint draft from the hallway door.

"Irene Årsby felt it was appropriate to contact you. We have a new Saturday night massacre for you. It looks absolutely hellish."

Cecilie crept up behind her to place a pink toweling dressing gown, adorned with a massive Harley-Davidson logo, over her shoulders.

"Whereabouts?"

"A workmen's hut belonging to the Moelven company, beside the River Lo. It had been secured with a little padlock, but a toddler could've managed to get in if he wanted to. You've no idea what it looks like in there."

"Oh, yes, I've some idea. Did you find anything interesting?"

"Nothing. Only blood. Everywhere. Do you want to see it?"

Detective Inspector Wilhelmsen wanted to see it. The blood-soaked scenes of non-existent crimes were beginning to intrigue her profoundly. On the other hand, although Cecilie's patience was well renowned, it was

35

not inexhaustible. A line had to be drawn.

"No, I'll content myself with the pictures this time. Thanks for phoning."

"No bother!"

Just as she was about to replace the receiver, she changed her mind in a flash.

"Hello! Are you still there?"

"Yes."

"Did you notice if there was anything written in the blood?"

"Yes, in fact. A number. Several digits. Pretty illegible, but it's been photographed from all angles."

"Excellent. That's actually quite important. Good night. And thanks again!"

"No problem!"

Hanne Wilhelmsen scuttled back to bed.

"Anything important?" Cecilie asked.

"No, only another of those pools of blood I told you about. Nothing serious."

A few minutes later, Hanne Wilhelmsen was drifting somewhere in the borderland between dreams and reality, on the point of falling asleep, when Cecilie dragged her back.

"How long are we going to continue with this phone system of ours?" She spoke softly into space, as though she didn't really anticipate a response.

It was just as well, for Hanne turned her

back on her without uttering a word. Suddenly the quilts, which had been lying more or less on top of each other, forming a shared cover over two people who belonged together, were imperceptibly drawn in their respective directions. Hanne tucked the quilt comfortably around herself, still without a sound.

"I can't understand this, Hanne. I've accepted it for many years. But you've always said that, someday, it would be different."

Still Hanne Wilhelmsen lay there, saying not a word, curled in a position with her back displaying icy rejection.

"Two phone numbers. I've never met any of your colleagues. Neither have I met your parents. Your sister is just somebody you mention now and again in a childhood story. We can't even spend Christmas together."

Cecilie was fully animated now and raised herself slightly in the bed. It was more than two years since she had last mentioned this topic, and although she had very little belief she would achieve anything at all, she suddenly felt an incredible urgency to express her opinion. She still hadn't resigned herself to this arrangement. She would never be content with the watertight bulkhead against everything that was Hanne's life outside their flat. Gingerly, she placed a hand on Hanne's spine, but removed it at once.

"Why are all our friends doctors and nurses? Why is it only me and my family we can associate with? God's truth, Hanne, I've never even spoken to any policeman other than you!"

"It's not 'policeman,'" came the muffled sound from the pillows.

Cecilie again tried to place her hand on the back blocking her, and this time she didn't need to pull it away. The entire body was shaking. Hanne Wilhelmsen had nothing to say. Remaining silent, Cecilie lay down beside her partner, pressing close to the sobbing woman, and decided there and then not to broach the subject again. At least not for many years.

SATURDAY, MAY 29

Later it struck her that he didn't look too bad. Tall and blond. Somewhat broad shouldered. A dull worn-out lightbulb above the entrance door confirmed that his hair was drawn back over the temples and he was uncommonly tanned for that time of year, even considering the fine weather. The woman's complexion was milky pale in the faint light, while he was bronze, as though the Easter ski season had just taken place.

She shrank from her own shadow and fumbled to find the keys in her voluminous fabric bag. He was paying careful attention with an interest she, strictly speaking, should have found worthy of note. It looked as though he had a wager with himself on whether she was capable of finding anything in all the jumble.

" 'Money's not everything in this world,' said the old man, when he looked into a lady's handbag! Can you manage to find anything?"

She treated the guy to a weary smile. She couldn't muster anything more. It was too late.

"Girls like you shouldn't be out at this time of night," he continued as she opened the door. He followed her inside.

"Sleep tight, then," he said, and disappeared upstairs.

The mailbox was empty. She didn't feel very well, either. She hadn't had much to drink, only a couple of half liters, but there was something about smoky premises. Her eyes were stinging, and her contact lenses felt as though they were glued firmly to her eyeballs.

The entire block had gone to sleep; only the distant bass of a powerful stereo system in a neighboring apartment block vibrated inaudibly under her feet.

There were two security locks on the door. You couldn't be careful enough — a single woman in the center of the city, her father reminded her often — and he had fitted them himself. She used only the one. A limit had to be placed on pessimism.

The warm, welcoming smell of home enveloped her as she stumbled across the threshold. When she was halfway through the door, he was there.

The shock was greater than the pain as she crashed to the floor. Behind her she heard the click of the lock. The cold, hard hand across her mouth paralyzed her completely. His knee pressed heavily and forcefully into the small of her back, and her head was yanked backward by the hair. Her back felt about to snap in two.

"Be really quiet, be a good girl, and everything will be fine."

His voice was different from three minutes before. But she knew it was him. And she knew what he was after. A twenty-four-year-old girl in a rented apartment in Oslo city center didn't have any valuables to speak of. Other than what he was looking for. She knew it.

But she didn't fear it. He could do what he wanted. If only he didn't kill her. It was death she was afraid of. Only death.

Everything went black because of the excruciating pain. Or was it perhaps because she hadn't taken a breath? Slowly he released his grip on her mouth, while repeating his instruction to keep quiet. It wasn't necessary. Her larynx had swollen into an enormous, aching, silent tumor, blocking everything.

Dear God, don't let me die. Don't let me die. Let him finish fast — fast, fast.

41

This was her single thought, churning around in her terrified brain like a maelstrom, over and over again.

He can do whatever he wants, but dear, dear God, don't let me die.

The tears came unbidden, a silent trickle as though her eyes were reacting on their own initiative. They were acting automatically without registering that she was not actually crying. Suddenly the man stood up. Her spine protested as it fell into its original position, and she now lay flat on her stomach. But not for long. He grabbed hold of her head, one hand on her right ear, the other in her hair, and dragged her into the living room. The pain was overwhelming, and she tried to scramble after him. He was going too fast, her arms couldn't manage to keep pace. Her neck stretched behind him in confusion, trying to avoid breaking right off. She blacked out again.

Dear God. Don't let me die.

He didn't switch on the light. A streetlamp directly outside the window afforded sufficient illumination. In the middle of the living room floor, he let go. Crouching in a fetal position, she began to cry in earnest. Quietly, but accompanied by sobs and shudders. She held her hands in front of her face, in a futile hope that the man would be gone

42

when she removed them.

All at once he was upon her again. A cloth was forced into her mouth. The dishcloth. The pungent taste almost choked her. She retched violently, but there was no way out for what came up from her stomach. Then she lost consciousness.

The cloth was gone when she awoke. She was lying in her own bed and felt naked. The man was lying on top of her. She could feel his penis thrusting in and out, but the pain around her ankles was more intense. Her feet were tied to each of the bedposts with something sharp; it felt like steel wire.

Dear, holy God. Don't let me die. I'll never complain about anything ever again.

She had given up. There was nothing she could do. She tried to scream, but her vocal cords were still immobilized.

"You're gorgeous," he hissed between his teeth. "A beautiful lady like you can't get through Saturday night without cock!"

His sweat dripped onto her face, searing her skin, and she twisted her head from side to side to avoid it. In a second he released one of her wrists to deliver a powerful smack on her ear.

"Lie still!"

It took time. How long, she had no idea. When he was finished, he remained lying on top of her like a lump of lead. He was panting. She said nothing, did nothing. It was as much as she could do to exist at all.

He rose slowly and loosened the moorings around her feet. It was steel wire. He must have brought it with him, she thought lethargically. There was nothing like that in her apartment. Although she was now free to move, she remained lying there, apathetic. He turned her onto her stomach. She offered no resistance.

He climbed on top of her again. For a sluggish second she realized he still had an erection. She couldn't comprehend how it was ready for use so soon, only a minute after his earlier orgasm.

He spread her buttocks. Then he took her from behind. She had nothing to say about it. She passed out yet again but managed to repeat her fervent prayer.

Dear, dear God in heaven. Don't let me die. I'm only twenty-four years old. Don't let me die.

He was gone. She hoped. She was still lying in the same position as when she had fainted, naked, on her stomach. Outside, the sounds of Sunday morning were just beginning to be heard. It was no longer night. A bright May morning was creeping into the room, lending her skin a bluish

44

tinge. She didn't dare to move so she could see the time on her bedside clock. Not moving a muscle, she kept lying there, listening to her own heartbeats. For three hours. Then she was almost certain. He must have left.

She stood up stiffly, looking down at her body. Her breasts were hanging lifelessly, as though bewailing her fate, or perhaps they were already dead. Her ankles had swollen enormously. A broad, jagged, bloody wound encircled each of her ankles. Her anus ached fiercely, and there was a throbbing sensation in her vagina reaching far up inside her belly. Calmly and firmly, almost impassive, she threw off the bedclothes. That didn't take much time, and she attempted to dump them in the garbage. The bin wasn't large enough, and, sobbing and increasingly enraged, she tried in vain to stuff them into the bag. She had to give up and sat there on the floor, totally shattered, naked and defenseless.

Dear God. Why couldn't you let me die instead?

The doorbell rang brutally through the apartment. It cut right through her, and she couldn't hold back a scream.

"Kristine?"

45

The voice was far, far away, but its anxiety sliced through the two doors.

"Go away," she mumbled, with no hope of him hearing.

"Kristine? Are you there?"

The voice was louder now and more distressed.

"GO AWAY!"

All the strength that hadn't been there during the night, when she really needed it, gathered itself into a single shriek.

Immediately afterward, he stood facing her, gasping for breath. He dropped his key ring on the floor.

"Kristine! My girl!"

He bent down, putting his arms tenderly around the naked, crumpled body. The man was trembling with fright, and his breath was fluttering like a rabbit's. She wanted to console him, say something to make it all better again, say everything was fine, nothing had happened. But when she felt the stiff material of his shirt brush against her face, and inhaled his reassuring, familiar male scent, she gave up hope.

Her giant of a father held her tight, rocking her from side to side like a little child. He knew what had happened. The garbage can with the overflowing bedsheets, the blood around her ankles, her naked, unpro-

46

tected figure, and the bewildered sobs he had never heard before. He lifted her carefully onto the sofa and wrapped the blanket around her. The coarse woolen fabric probably chafed against her skin, but he didn't want to let her go to fetch a sheet. Instead he made a sacred vow to himself as he stroked her hair repeatedly.

But he said nothing.

Monday, May 31

It was difficult to become accustomed to them. The twenty-four-year-old woman sitting facing her, eyes downcast, was Detective Inspector Hanne Wilhelmsen's forty-second rape victim. She kept count. Rape was the worst crime of all. Killing was something different. Murder she could in a way understand. A crazy, furious moment of violence and volatility, perhaps pent-up aggression going back years. That she could almost wrap her head around. But not rape.

The victim had brought her father with her. That was not so unusual. A father, a friend, sometimes a partner, though seldom a mother. Oddly enough. Perhaps a mother was too close.

The man was massive and looked out of place in the narrow chair. He was not actually overweight, simply large. In any case, the extra kilos suited him. He had to be more than six foot three, with a solid appearance, robustly masculine and somewhat ugly. One enormous hand was placed on his daughter's slender one. They resembled each other in some indefinable way. The woman had a totally different build, almost skinny, although she had inherited her father's height. However, there was something about the eyes, the same shape, the same color. And with exactly the same expression. A helpless, sorrowful aspect that in fact, surprisingly enough, was more striking in the case of the huge man.

Detective Inspector Hanne Wilhelmsen felt embarrassed. Rape was something she never got used to. But Hanne was smart, and smart police officers don't show their feelings. At least not when they are embarrassed.

"I have to ask you some questions," she said softly. "Some of them are not so pleasant. May I proceed?"

The father squirmed in his seat.

"She was questioned for several hours yesterday," he said. "Is it really necessary to go over it all again?"

"Yes, unfortunately. The report isn't yet comprehensive."

She hesitated imperceptibly.

"We can wait till tomorrow, but . . ."

She tugged at her hair.

"But it's fairly urgent for us, you understand. It's vital to be fast in an investigation such as this."

"It's fine."

The woman answered for herself this time. Changing position slightly, she braced herself for yet another reiteration of Saturday night.

"It's absolutely fine," she repeated, this time directing herself to her father.

Now the daughter's hand comforted her father's.

He's damn well got the worst of it, were the detective inspector's thoughts as she started on the interview.

"Lunch, Håkon?"

"No thanks, I've eaten already."

Hanne Wilhelmsen glanced at the clock.

"Already? It's only eleven o'clock!"

"Yes, but I'll come with you for a coffee. Keep you company. The canteen or the office?"

"The office."

It struck him as soon as he entered. She had new curtains. They weren't exactly police regulation. Periwinkle blue with meadow flowers.

"They're really nice! How did you manage that?"

She didn't reply, instead fetching a bundle of neatly folded material from the cupboard.

"Sewed some for you as well."

He was dumbfounded.

"It cost only seven kroner a meter. At Ikea. Seven kroner a meter! At any rate, they're much more appealing, and far cleaner, than those state-issued rags over there!"

She pointed at a filthy gray curtain, dumped in the wastepaper basket, that seemed embarrassed at being mentioned.

"Thanks very much!"

Police Attorney Håkon Sand accepted the pile of material with enthusiasm, immediately spilling his entire cup of coffee over it. A large brown flower bloomed among all the little sprigs of red and pink. With an almost inaudible long-suffering sigh, the female detective inspector reclaimed the curtains.

"I'll launder them."

"No, not at all, I'll do it myself!"

There was a scent of unfamiliar perfume in the office. Unfamiliar, and slightly over-powering. The explanation lay in a slim green folder on the desk between them.

"By the way, this is our case," she said, when she had finished cleaning the worst of the coffee damage. She passed him the papers.

"Rape. Dreadful."

"All rapes are dreadful," the police attorney mumbled. Having read for a few moments, he concurred. It was horrendous.

"How did she seem?"

"An all right kind of girl. Rather sweet. Decent in every way. Medical student. Smart. Successful. And very raped."

She gave herself a shake.

"They sit there, timid and helpless, looking at the floor and twiddling their thumbs as though it were their fault. I get so discouraged. I feel even more helpless than they do, sometimes. So I think."

"How do you think I feel, then?" Håkon Sand said. "At least you're a woman. It's not your fault men commit rape."

He dropped the two interview reports regarding the medical student onto the desk.

"Well, it's not exactly your fault either, you know." The detective inspector smiled.

"No . . . But I feel quite ill at ease when I have to relate to them. Poor girls. But . . ."

He stretched his arms above his head, yawned and drank the rest of his coffee.

"But I avoid seeing them, most of the time. The public prosecutor attends to those cases. Fortunately. For me, the girls are merely names on a piece of paper. Have you taken your bike out yet, by the way?"

Hanne Wilhelmsen smiled broadly as she got to her feet.

"Come here." She waved her arm, positioning herself beside the window. "There! The rose-colored one!"

"Have you got a pink bike?"

"It's not pink," she said, offended. "It's rose. Or cerise. But certainly not pink."

Grinning, Håkon Sand poked her vigorously in the side.

"A pink Harley-Davidson! The worst thing I've ever seen!"

He looked her up and down.

"On the other hand, you're altogether too attractive to be riding a motorbike at all. At the very least, it would have to be a pink one."

For the very first time since they had met almost four years previously, he saw Detective Inspector Hanne Wilhelmsen's cheeks turn bright red. He pointed triumphantly at her face.

"Pink!"

The lemonade bottle hit him in the middle of the chest. Fortunately, it was made of plastic.

She couldn't for the life of her give a

particularly detailed description of the rapist. Inside her head, somewhere or other, the picture was absolutely clear, but she couldn't manage to extract it.

The police artist was a patient man. Sketching and erasing, he outlined features afresh and suggested a different chin. The woman shook her head, squinting at the portrait, and requested he take a little more off the ears. Nothing helped. It did not resemble him in the least.

They had been at this for three hours. The artist had to take a new sheet of paper four times, and was about to give up. The drawings were placed in front of her, none of them complete.

"Which one looks most like him, then?"

"None of them . . ."

It was time to give it a rest.

Detective Inspector Hanne Wilhelmsen and Police Attorney Håkon Sand weren't the only ones who didn't like rape cases. Chief Inspector Kaldbakken, Hanne Wilhelmsen's immediate superior, was bloody sick of them too. His equine face reacted as though he had been presented with a bag of spoiled oats and wanted more than anything else to say no, thanks for offering.

"The sixth in less than a fortnight," he

mumbled. "Though this one here has a slightly different method. The other five are self-inflicted. But not this one."

Self-inflicted rapes . . . the description infuriated her. There were more than enough of such cases: girls who had gone home with men who were more or less strangers to them after a liquor-soaked night on the town. Post-party rapes. Rarely did anything come of these cases. One person's word against another's. All the same, they were hardly a girl's own fault. But she chose not to say anything. Not because she was scared of her boss but because she simply couldn't be bothered.

"The victim hasn't been able to help much with a drawing," she said instead. "And she can't spot the guy in our archives either. Frustrating."

It was true. Not first and foremost because they wouldn't solve the case. As far as that was concerned, it was in good company. However, the actual modus operandi gave them grounds for disquiet.

"Men like that don't give up until they're caught."

Kaldbakken scanned the room without fixing his eyes on anything. Neither of them spoke, but they both sensed a hint of foreboding in the glorious May sunshine that

55

lay enticingly outside the unwashed windows. The skinny man rapped a crooked finger on the folder.

"This chap could give us a hot time of it this spring," he declared, extremely concerned. "I'm going to suggest dropping the other five cases. We prioritize this one. Give it top priority, Wilhelmsen. Yes indeed, men like that! Top priority."

The room was so overheated that even her flimsy worn-out sweater with the Washington Redskins logo emblazoned on the front was too much. She yanked it over her head. The undershirt beneath was wet between her breasts, and she tugged it a little, to no avail. The window was open wide, but she had to keep the door closed. The cross breeze wouldn't be a good idea for the modicum of tidiness she had managed to achieve on her desk.

There wasn't much she could do. Sure enough, they had found some evidence at the crime scene, a couple of hairs that might belong to the perpetrator, a few bloodstains that probably weren't his, and some traces of semen that definitely were. With merely a poor sketch, there was little to be gained through the mass media, though they would give it a try. Showing the photographs hadn't led to anything either.

It would take time to obtain an analysis of the sparse forensic material. In the meantime, there was little to do other than interview the neighbors to discover whether they had seen or heard anything. That was unlikely. They never had.

She pressed four buttons on the intercom.

"Erik?"

"Yes?"

"It's Hanne here. Do you have time to come with me on a little jaunt?"

Erik did indeed. He was Hanne Wilhelmsen's puppy dog, the first-year constable with red hair and freckles that covered his face. Three seconds later he presented himself at her door, wagging his tail.

"Should I get a car?"

She rose to her feet, smiling broadly, and threw a black crash helmet in his direction. He caught it with an even broader smile.

"Ace!"

Hanne Wilhelmsen shook her head.

"Cool, Erik. Not ace, cool."

The building was probably from the turn of the century. It was situated in the west end and had been renovated with great care. Quite the opposite of the looming apartment blocks to the east, screeching at each other in lilac and pink and other colors hardly even invented when the buildings were new. This apartment block was pearl gray. The windows and doors had a border of dark blue, and the refurbishment must have been fairly recent.

Hanne Wilhelmsen parked her bike on the sidewalk. Erik the Red hopped off before her in a flurry of excitement and perspiration.

"Can we take a detour on the road home?"

"We'll see."

The doorbell at the entrance had two columns with five names in each. On the first floor lived K. Håverstad, sensible and gender neutral. The precaution hadn't helped her greatly. On the ground floor, someone must have moved in recently. The corresponding nameplate had not been inserted behind glass in accordance with the regulations like the others, but instead stuck on with a piece of tape. An exotic-sounding name, the only one in the entire block giving any indication of foreign origins. Detective Inspector Wilhelmsen rang the doorbell of the neighbor living across the landing from K. Håverstad.

"Hello?"

The voice belonged to a man. An extremely old man.

She introduced herself. The man seemed overjoyed to receive visitors and kept his finger on the door-release button until they were well on their way upstairs. When they reached the first floor, he was standing there to greet them with outstretched hands and a big smile, as though they were arriving for a party.

"Come in, come in," he wheezed, holding the door wide open.

He had to be almost ninety and barely more than five foot three. His back was hunched, making it essential to sit before they had any hope of eye contact.

The sun-drenched living room was clean and tidy, and dominated by two enormous birdcages. A large colorful parrot was sitting in each cage, making an infernal racket. There were green houseplants everywhere, and old paintings with massive gilt frames hung on the walls. The brick-hard settee was uncomfortable. Erik, not quite sure what to do, remained standing beside one of the parrots.

"Just a moment, and I'll make some coffee!"

The old man was over the moon. Hanne tried to ward off the coffee, but it was no use. Porcelain cups and a dainty stemmed cake dish were placed in front of them.

Once bitten, twice shy: she said no thanks to the cakes but ventured a half cup of coffee. Police Constable Erik was not so experienced and helped himself with gusto. One bite was enough. A perplexed expression spread across his eyes, and he looked around in desperation for a place to get rid of the three slices he had lavished on his own plate. Unable to find any way out, he spent the remainder of the visit trying to force down the pieces of cake.

"You may know why we're here?"

The man didn't reply to the detective inspector's question, instead simply smiling, trying to palm her off with a slice of marzipan cake.

"We're from the police," she said, louder this time.

"The police, yes."

He was smirking.

"The police. Nice young folk. Nice girl."

The old fogey's hand, wrinkled and dry as dust, had surprisingly soft skin, and he stroked the back of her hand several times. Calmly, she took his hand and met his gaze. His eyes were light blue, so pale they almost merged into the whites of his eyeballs. His eyebrows were ferocious, raised in an optimistic curve where the hairs were longest, in the middle. They looked like little horns.

A pleasant and kindly disposed, diminutive devil.

"There was a crime in my neighbor's apartment! On Saturday night!"

She gave a start when an echo sounded from one of the cages.

"Saturday night, Saturday night!"

Erik got even more of a fright. He had the parrot right at his ear and dropped the cake dish on the floor. Distressed about the damage but delighted the remaining piece of cake was now lying among the shards of porcelain on the floor so he couldn't reasonably be expected to devour it, he excused himself, mouth full and stuttering.

The old man was as cheerful as ever. He hobbled off to fetch a dustpan and brush. Erik followed after him, insisting on clearing it up himself. The owner of the parrots placed two large black cloths over the cages, and there was sudden silence.

"So. Now we can talk. You don't need to speak so loudly. I can hear fine."

They sat down again, facing each other.

"A crime," he mumbled softly. "A felony. There's so much of that these days. In the newspapers. Every day. I stay indoors most of the time."

"That's probably for the best," the police-

61

woman acknowledged. "The safest thing to do."

The room was hot. A mantel clock was ticking loudly, slowly, and as she sat there waiting she realized it was almost four o'clock. Hesitantly and laboriously, it struck four hollow chimes.

"We're here to check with the neighbors. To see if they saw or heard anything," Hanne said.

"There's something wrong with that clock. It wasn't like that before. The sound has changed. Don't you think so?"

Hanne Wilhelmsen sighed. "A bit difficult to say. I haven't heard it before. But I agree, it sounds slightly . . . slightly unhappy. Perhaps you should get a watchmaker to have a look at it?"

Perhaps he didn't agree. He didn't say anything and simply continued to sit there shaking his head.

"Did you hear . . . Sir, did you hear anything on Saturday night? Early yesterday morning?"

Despite the old man's statement about his hearing, she couldn't prevent herself raising her voice.

"No, hear anything . . . I don't think so. I really heard nothing. Other than what I hear every night, of course. Cars. And then the tram, when it goes past. But it doesn't do that during the night, of course. So I wouldn't have heard that."

"Do you usually —"

"I sleep very lightly, you see," he interrupted. "It's as though I've done all my sleeping through my whole long life. I'm eighty-nine now. My wife only lived to sixty-seven. Here, have another piece of cake. My daughter baked it. No, as a matter of fact it was my granddaughter. I get a bit mixed up now and again. My daughter's dead, of course! She can't very well have baked any cakes!"

He offered an unassuming, serene smile, as though in sudden recognition that time had not merely caught up with him but had long ago passed him by.

Waste of time. Detective Inspector Hanne Wilhelmsen finished her coffee, thanked him graciously, and drew the conversation to a close.

"What kind of crime are we talking about?" he asked, suddenly interested as the two police officers clutched their helmets and leather jackets in the hallway beside the outer door.

Detective Inspector Wilhelmsen turned to face him and hesitated for a moment about bothering the dear old man with the city's

63

brutal dark side. Then she checked herself. He's seen three times more of life than I have.

"Rape. It was a rape."

He shivered, spreading his arms expressively.

"And that lovely young girl," he said. "So terrible."

Closing the door behind them, the old man shuffled off to rejoin his feathered friends and remove the cloths from the cages. He was rewarded by a cacophony of thanks and stuck his finger in at one of the birds, and was met with a friendly nibble.

"Rape. That's dreadful," he said to the parrot, who nodded, totally in agreement. "Could there be someone here in the block who might think of doing such a thing? No, it really must have been an outsider. Perhaps it was the fellow in the red car. I hadn't seen that one before." He withdrew his finger and padded over to a well-worn, comfortable armchair at the window. This was where he usually sat when sleepless nights drove him out of his warm, cozy bed. The city was his friend, as long as he was sitting safely indoors. He had lived in the same apartment all his life, watching as horses and carts were replaced by noisy motorcars, gas lamps disappeared as they were overtaken by the advantages of electric lights, and cobblestones were covered over by dark-gray asphalt. He knew his neighborhood well, at least as far as he could see from his window on the first floor. He knew which cars belonged here and who owned them. The red car was one he hadn't seen before. Neither had he known the tall, well-built young man who had driven off in the early hours either. It must have been him.

He stayed sitting there for a while, dozing. Then he padded noiselessly through to the kitchen to heat some broth.

None of the other neighbors had heard anything. Or seen anything. Most of them had noticed the police presence on Sunday morning. Rumors had circulated in the apartment block, and they had all picked up a great deal more than the dear old man on the first floor. There was nothing, however, of interest to the police: only anecdotes the residents had heard from one another, impassioned tales over the stairway railings, with lots of head-shaking and disbelief, speculation and reciprocal assurances they would all have to be more vigilant in the future.

Kristine Håverstad was not at home. Hanne Wilhelmsen knew that. Nevertheless, she rang the bell for safety's sake, waiting a few seconds before letting herself in. She had been given the keys by the young woman, who had told Hanne that she was moving home to her father's for a while. For how long, she didn't know.

The apartment was tidy, clean and snug. It was not large, so the two officers made a quick survey: a living room with a semi-open plan kitchen layout and a moderately large bedroom with a work desk in one corner. The rooms were accessed from an oblong hallway, so narrow it could almost be considered merely a corridor. The bathroom was so tiny it must be possible to sit on the toilet, shower, and brush one's teeth at the same time. It was spotless, with a faint scent of pine bleach.

Forensics had been there, and Hanne Wilhelmsen knew she wouldn't find anything of significance. She was simply curious. The bedclothes were gone, but the quilt lay tidily in place. It was not a double bed, but neither was it so narrow there wasn't room for two good friends. It was made of pine, with a little decorative bed knob at the top of each bedpost. Directly below the two at the foot of the bed she could see dark, uneven ridges. She squatted down and let her finger slide around the indentation.

Minuscule splinters of wood pierced her finger. Sighing deeply, she left the bedroom and stood in the living room doorway.

"What are we looking for?" Erik asked tentatively.

"Nothing," Detective Inspector Hanne Wilhelmsen replied, looking vacantly into space to emphasize her point.

"We're not looking for anything. I'm just having a look at this apartment where Kristine Håverstad will never again be able to stay."

"It's bloody awful," muttered the young lad.

"It's more than that," Hanne said. "It's far, far more than that."

Locking the door behind them with both security locks, they took the long way along the main ring road back to the station. Red-haired Erik was elated. By the end of the journey he didn't know which he was more in love with: Hanne Wilhelmsen or her big rose-colored Harley.

TUESDAY, JUNE 1

Kristine Håverstad was trying to pluck up
courage but couldn't quite summon the effort. It was all the same to her. She did not
need a lawyer. She didn't really need anything at all. She simply wanted to stay at
home, at home with her father. She wanted
to lock all the doors and watch television.
In any case, she didn't want to have an attorney, but the detective inspector had
insisted. She had shown her a list with the
names of what she had called "counsel for
the injured party" and cautiously indicated
that Linda Løvstad would be a good choice.
When she had nodded, shrugging her shoulders, Hanne Wilhelmsen had phoned on her
behalf. Kristine Håverstad could come to
lawyer Løvstad's office as soon as ten thirty
the following morning.

Now she was standing outside the given
address, trying to steel herself. The plaque
bore scars where attorneys' names had been

scored out, but it was clear nonetheless. "Lawyers Andreassen, Bugge, Hoel, and Løvstad, first floor." Black lettering on shabby brass.

A dog approached her, wagging its tail, when she opened the glass door on the first floor. She flinched but was reassured by a man who couldn't possibly be a lawyer, judging by his attire. Threadbare jeans and sneakers. Smiling, he caught hold of the dog's collar and scolded the animal on his way into an office. Inside a long corridor lay another dog, a hulk of charcoal gray, with head in paws and mournful expression, as though demonstrating heartfelt sympathy for her ordeal. A slim, smartly dressed young woman at a combined switchboard and reception desk pointed her along the corridor toward the sad gray dog.

"The second to last door on the left," she said, smiling, in a quiet voice.

"Come in," she heard before she had even managed to knock.

Perhaps the man with the first dog had been a lawyer after all. Linda Løvstad wasn't wearing sneakers but flip-flops and jeans, and a blouse Kristine recognized from the Hennes & Mauritz department store. The office did not flaunt any notably luxurious features either. What's more, there was a third dog in an alcove. Perhaps it was a precondition for working here. Owning a dog. This one was a mongrel, skinny, ugly, and coal black, with big, beautiful eyes.

A massive curved work desk dominated the space. The simple bookshelves were sparsely filled, and on the floor, leaning against the built-in shelving, sat an enormous, comical stuffed cloth cat. It wasn't pretty, and not especially amusing either, but combined with a toy police car, cheap pictures in clip frames, and impatiens in a white flowerpot, it contributed to making the place less intimidating.

Standing up, the lawyer stretched out her hand as Kristine complied with her invitation to enter. She was tall and skinny as a rake, and flat as a board, with thin, flyaway pale blonde hair trying without success to appear thicker, piled up into some kind of topknot. Her face, however, was friendly, her smile attractive, and her handshake firm. She offered coffee, then picked up an empty light-brown folder and made a start by writing down her personal details.

Kristine Håverstad had no idea what she was doing there. Under no circumstances would she be able to go through the whole explanation one more time.

The woman was a mind reader.

"You don't need to tell me about the actual rape," she reassured her. "I'll get the documentation from the police."

A silence ensued, though not uncomfortable. It was actually soothing. The lawyer looked at Kristine with a smile, leafing through some papers that couldn't relate to her, perhaps waiting for her to say something. Kristine remained sitting, her eyes on the stuffed cat, rubbing the arm of her chair. When the attorney still made no sign of speaking, Kristine shrugged her shoulders imperceptibly and looked down at the floor.

"Are you getting help? Psychologist or something similar?"

"Sure. Or, it's a social worker, actually. Just as good."

"Is it helping?"

"Doesn't feel like it at the moment. But I know it's important. From a long-term point of view, I think. So far I've only been to her once, though. Yesterday."

Attorney Løvstad nodded encouragingly.

"My role is really somewhat limited. I'll act as a kind of link between you and the police. If there's anything you're wondering about, then you just get in touch with me. The police will continue to keep me informed. They're not usually very conscientious about that, but you've been very

71

fortunate with your investigating officer. She usually follows things up."

Now they were both smiling.

"Yes, she seems nice," her client acknowledged.

"And then I'll help you with compensation."

The young woman looked bewildered. "Compensation?"

"Yes, you're entitled to compensation. Either from the rapist, or from the state. There are special arrangements for that sort of thing."

"I'm not interested in any kind of compensation!"

Kristine Håverstad was taken aback by her own extreme reaction. Compensation? As though anyone at anytime could give her a sum of money large enough to make amends for all the unpleasantness and wipe out that horrific night that had turned her whole life upside down. Money?

"I don't want anything!"

If her tear ducts hadn't been completely exhausted, she would have started to weep. She did not want money. If she could make a choice, she would want to have a video player with her life available on a recording. She would then rewind the days and go home to her father last Saturday instead of being destroyed in her own apartment. But she did not have the choice.

Her bottom lip, and then her entire chin, was shaking uncontrollably.

Her final words were spat out like tainted food.

"Easy there."

The lawyer leaned forward, across the enormous desktop, and caught her eye.

"We can talk about all this later. Maybe you'll still feel the same about it then, and in that case no one will force you, of course. Perhaps you'll change your mind. We'll leave it for now. Is there anything you need help with at the moment? Anything at all?"

The tall, slender woman gazed at her victim support counsel for several static seconds. Then she couldn't endure any more. She stretched out across the desk with her arms around her head. Her hair fell forward to hide her face. She sobbed for half an hour of tearless grief while the lawyer could do nothing other than stroke her client on the back and whisper words of reassurance.

"If only someone could help me," gasped the young woman. "And if only someone could help my dad."

At long last she sat up again.

"I don't really want anything to do with

the police. I'm not bothered whether they capture the man who did it. All I want . . ."

She was overcome by sobs again, but this time she remained upright.

"I just want some help. And somebody to help my father. He doesn't speak to me. He's around me all the time, doesn't know what he can do to help, but he . . . he says nothing. I'm afraid he might . . ."

Then she was overcome again. After another quarter of an hour, for the very first time in her relatively short legal career, Linda Løvstad had to call an ambulance to come and collect her client.

They hadn't much faith in the drawing but had printed it regardless. This had led to something, at least, and now they had more than fifty tip-offs about named persons. Perhaps that was precisely because the sketch was so devoid of character: indistinct features, a vague face, a shadow picture with no identity.

Detective Inspector Hanne Wilhelmsen held out the newspaper on outstretched arms, tilting her head.

"It could be anyone at all," she declared. "With a bit of imagination, it might be four or five different men I know."

Squinting, she turned her head to the

other side.

"It looks like you, Håkon! It damn well looks like you too!"

She laughed and let him tear the newspaper out of her hands.

"It most certainly does not," he protested, feeling insulted. "I don't have such a round face. My eyes aren't so close together either. And besides, I've got more hair."

The newspaper was crumpled ferociously and thrown into the bin.

"If this is the way you're conducting this investigation, I can well understand why no one has any hope of solving it," he declared, still somewhat miffed. "Honestly . . ."

She didn't give up. She retrieved the crushed newspaper, smoothing it flat with a long-fingered, slender hand, nails lacquered with clear enamel.

"Look at this likeness. Couldn't it be anyone at all? These drawings really shouldn't be publicized. Either the victim fixates on some particular blemish, so the man is given a nose that's far too large and we get no tip-offs. Or else they look like this. Like a man. A Norwegian man."

They stared for a long time at the picture of the anonymous Norwegian man with the insignificant face.

"Do we actually know he's Norwegian?"

"Not with absolute certainty, but he spoke fluently and looked Norwegian. We have to assume he is."

"But he was supposedly quite tanned . . ."

"Now you really must give over, Håkon. There are enough racists here in the force without you persuading yourself to believe a blond man speaking in Oslo dialect is a Moroccan."

"But they commit rape far mo—"

"Cut it out, Håkon."

Her tone was almost aggressive now. It was true that North Africans were over-represented in the rape statistics. It was true the rapes of which they were found guilty were often unusually vicious. It was also true she found her own prejudices surfacing occasionally, as a result of too many encounters with curly-haired, handsome scumbags who lied to your face even when they'd been caught literally with their trousers down and every single Norwegian man in the same situation would have said something else: yes, true enough, we were fucking, but it was of her own free will. She knew all that, but it was quite another thing to say it out loud.

"What do you think are the hidden statistics for 'Norwegian' rapes?"

She waved two fingers of each hand in the

air when she used the word "Norwegian."

"Those rapes that happen after a night on the town, at office parties, by husbands . . . you name it! That's where you'll find the hidden statistics. Every girl knows they're hopeless to prosecute. While the more 'straightforward' rapes . . ."

Her fingers waved in the air again.

". . . the nasty assaults, the dreadful dark-skinned attackers, the ones who aren't from here, the ones everybody knows the police are out to get . . . they're the ones that are reported."

Silence. Feeling offended, Håkon smiled, shame-faced and defensive.

"I didn't mean it like that."

"No, I realize that. But you really shouldn't say such things. Not even as a joke. Of one thing I'm absolutely sure."

Sweaty and dispirited, she stood up, leaned across toward the window, and endeavored to open it wider. The new curtains fluttered slightly, more from her own movements than any draft from outside.

"God Almighty, it's scorching."

It was no use. The window slid back to a gap of ten centimeters, no good at all. It had to be thirty degrees Celsius in here.

"Of one thing I'm absolutely sure," she

repeated. "If all the rapes actually committed in this country were reported, we would all be horrified by two things."

Håkon Sand wasn't sure why she stopped. Perhaps to afford him the opportunity to guess what two things would horrify everyone. Instead of taking the chance of saying something stupid yet again, he waited for the upshot of her silence.

"First of all: how many rapes take place. Second: foreigners would feature in the statistics to almost exactly the same extent as their proportion of the population would suggest. Neither more nor less."

She moaned again about the heat.

"If these sweltering temperatures don't come to an end soon, I'll go crazy. I think I'll go out for a jaunt. Want to come?"

With a look of horror, he turned down her offer point-blank. Another motorcycle trip was still fresh in his memory: a freezing, dangerous journey through Vestfold in the late autumn six months previously, with Hanne Wilhelmsen in the driver's seat and himself as a blinded, soaking-wet pillion passenger. On that occasion, the excursion had been a matter of life or death. His first motorbike ride — and most decidedly his last.

"No thanks, I'd rather go and jump in the

lake," he said. It was half past four. They could actually go home.

"Strictly speaking, you should make a start on going through the tip-offs," he added meekly.

"I'll do that tomorrow, Håkon. Tomorrow."

He was consumed by despair. It was sitting like a nasty gray rat gnawing inside him, somewhere behind his breastbone. Since Sunday morning, he'd drunk two bottles of orange-flavored antacid to no avail. The rat obviously liked the taste and continued gnawing with renewed vigor. No matter what he did, no matter what he said, nothing was of any help. His daughter did not want to talk to him. True enough, she wanted to be there, in her own childhood home, sleeping in her childhood bedroom. He found a tiny scrap of comfort in that, the fact that she probably was at least finding some kind of security through keeping him close. But then she wouldn't talk.

He had collected Kristine from the emergency psychiatric clinic. When he saw her sitting there, exhausted, with dark eyes and sunken shoulders, she reminded him of his wife twenty years earlier. At that time, the young woman had sat like that, with the

79

same vacant stare, the same hopeless demeanor and expression-less mouth. She had just heard she would die, leaving behind her husband and daughter, barely four years old. Then, he'd become furious. He had cursed and yelled and taken his wife to see every single expert in the entire country. Eventually, he'd borrowed a considerable sum of money from his parents in a futile hope that distant experts in the United States, the promised land for all medical practitioners, would be able to alter the cruel diagnosis so mournfully reached by fourteen Norwegian doctors. The journey didn't result in anything other than the young woman dying far from home, and he spent the return trip with his beloved in a refrigerated compartment in the aircraft hold.

Single parenthood with little Kristine had been difficult. He had been newly qualified as a dentist, at a time when the previously lucrative profession had become less profitable after twenty years of social democratic public dental services. But they had managed. The middle of the seventies had seen the struggle for women's liberation, something, paradoxically enough, that had been of assistance to him. A single father insisting on looking after his daughter was favored by all kinds of special arrangements from the public authorities, great sympathy from everyone he came into contact with, as well as help and support from female colleagues and neighbors. They had managed.

There hadn't been many women. An occasional relationship, certainly, but never of particularly lengthy duration. Kristine had seen to that. On the three occasions he had ventured to introduce the topic of remarriage, she had sulked, rejecting every effort to curry favor. And she always won. He loved his daughter. Naturally, he understood that all men love their children, and from a purely rational viewpoint saw he wasn't especially different from the rest of the Norwegian male population. Emotionally, nevertheless, he insisted to himself and his circle of acquaintances that the relationship between himself and his daughter was a special one. They had only each other. He had been both father and mother to her. He had tended her in sickness, made sure she had freshly laundered clothes, and consoled the teenager when her first romance collapsed after three weeks. When the thirteen-year-old, in joy mixed with terror, showed him her bloodstained underpants, he was the one who took her to a restaurant for fillet steak accompanied by diluted red wine to celebrate his little daughter being on her way to becoming a woman. For two years, he had turned down every insistent demand for a brassiere, since the midge bites to be covered by the garment were so insignificant any bra at all would have looked comical. He had taken lonely pleasure in his daughter's brilliant school grades, and was alone with his bitter sorrow when she chose to celebrate with friends four years later when she was accepted into medical school in Oslo.

He loved his daughter, but he couldn't manage to reach her. When he collected her, she accompanied him willingly, and she had asked the emergency doctor to phone him. So she had wanted to go home. To him. However, she said nothing. Tentatively, he had fumbled for her hand in the car on the drive home, and she had allowed him to take it. Nevertheless, there was no response, just a limp hand passively accepting his grasp. Not a word was uttered. When they arrived home, he had tried to tempt her with a meal: freshly baked bread, sandwich toppings he knew she liked, roast beef and prawn salad, and the best red wine he possessed. She had seized the wine but left the food. After three glasses, she took the remainder of the bottle with her, excusing herself politely and heading for her bedroom.

That had been three hours ago. Not a sound was to be heard from her room. He rose to his feet, stiff from sitting on the sofa. It was American — low, excessively soft, and plump. The candles, palely flickering during the bright spring evening, were now sputtering, as they ran out of wax. Stopping at the door of the girl's bedroom, he stood stock-still for several minutes before daring to knock. There was no response. Hesitating for a few more minutes, he made up his mind to leave her in peace.

He went to bed.

In her girlish bedroom, painted yellow and adorned with checked curtains, Kristine Håverstad sat with a teddy bear on her lap and an empty wineglass in front of her on a white-painted table. Her bed was narrow, and she had cramps in her legs from having assumed a lotus position for a long time. She welcomed the cramps. They became increasingly uncomfortable, and she concentrated on examining how sore she actually was. Everything else receded, and all she could feel was the tingling, aching protest from limbs deprived of blood for a lengthy period. Eventually she could not endure it and lay down on the bed to stretch her legs. Even more excruciating when the sensation rushed back into her calves. She grabbed around one thigh with both hands, squeezing hard until tears pricked her eyes. All this to make the spasms last. She certainly couldn't continue like this, however.

After a while she let go, and the pain in her chest returned. It was completely empty inside, an enormous hollow space with an indefinable ache. It swirled around and around, faster and faster, and in the end she stood up to fetch the little box of pills prescribed by the emergency doctor. Valium, 2 mg. A tiny packet. Each pill represented hope of respite, to some degree. For a spell. She stood for ages holding the box in her left hand, then carried it to the bathroom, lifted the toilet seat, and poured pills down into the pale blue chlorinated water. They remained floating on the surface, bobbing gently, before slowly sinking one by one to the porcelain depths and disappearing. She flushed the toilet. Twice. Then she washed her face thoroughly in bracingly cold water before entering the living room. It was dark now. Only a tiny light on the television set was visible, shedding a pale yellow glow on the soft rugs at the entrance to the room. She picked up another bottle of red wine

84

from the kitchen, quietly, so as not to wake her father. If he was sleeping. She remained sitting in the best chair, her father's old armchair, until that bottle was empty too.

Then he appeared at the doorway. A towering figure, with slumped shoulders and the palms of his hands opened, outstretched from his pajama-clad body, in a gesture of helplessness. Neither of them said anything. He hesitated for a long time, eventually stepping into the room and crouching down beside her.

"Kristine," he said gently, to say something rather than because he had something to say. "Kristine. My girl."

She wanted so much to respond. More than anything else in the whole world, she wished she could engage with him, lean forward and let herself be comforted, and comfort him. Tell him sorry for what she had inflicted on him, sorry she had disappointed him and spoiled everything for him by being so stupid as to go off and get herself raped. She wished she could wipe out the last few horrendous days, wipe out everything, be eight years old and happy again, allowing herself to be tossed in the air and caught in his arms. But she simply couldn't. Nothing and no one could make everything all right again. She had destroyed his life. All she could manage to do was reach out her hand and let her little finger stroke his face, from the soft skin below the temple, across his rough, unshaven cheek until it rested at the cleft in his chin.

"Daddy," she said in almost a whisper and stood up. Staggering slightly, she regained her balance and returned to her room. At the door, she half turned and saw he was still there, crouched down, with his face in his hands. She closed the door behind her and lay fully clothed on her bed. After only a few minutes, she was in a deep and dreamless sleep.

WEDNESDAY, JUNE 2

The paved incline leading from Grønlandsleiret to Oslo police headquarters bustled
with activity. People were coming and going. A few taxis were driving up and down
at speed, dodging everything from men in
suits on their way to meetings with important people on the floors above to old ladies
tottering in on skinny legs, wearing sensible
walking shoes, to give irate and agitated
reports about missing poodles. The sun
shone incessantly, and the dandelions on
the grass were becoming gray haired. Even
Oslo Prison looked attractive in the midst
of the avenue of poplar trees, as though the
infamous TV crook Egon Olsen might
emerge from the gate at any moment, humming a tune, ready to plan another heist.
Half-naked people were sprawled or seated
in every possible spot between the buildings, some on their lunch hour, others
unemployed or housewives deriving pleasure

from the only patch of green in the Gamle Oslo quarter of the city. A few dark-skinned lads played soccer, startling the occasional sunbather with an errant ball to the stomach. The children laughed and showed no sign of shifting their match to another location.

Hanne Wilhelmsen and Håkon Sand were sitting on a bench directly beside the wall. Hanne had rolled her trousers up above her knees and removed her shoes. With a stolen glance, Håkon ascertained that she didn't shave her legs. It was okay, as she had only some light, soft, feminine down that made her look even lovelier than if her legs had been shiny. Her skin had already turned a shade of pale golden brown.

"Have you thought about one thing?" Håkon Sand inquired, food in mouth. He continued chewing and then folded the waxed paper neatly, pouring the rest of the milk carton contents down his throat.

"Have you considered that there wasn't a Saturday night massacre this time? I mean last Saturday night."

"Yes."

Detective Inspector Hanne Wilhelmsen had finished her modest lunch long before. It had consisted of yogurt and a medium-sized carrot. Incredulous, Håkon had asked her if she was on a diet, and she had not replied.

"Yes, I've thought about it," she acknowledged once more. "Odd. Perhaps the jokers have grown tired of it. We have at least managed to keep the story out of the newspapers. It must be a bit boring after a while, going to all that bother just to annoy us. He was probably hoping for something more. If the theory about it being a prankster is true, that is."

"Maybe he's quite simply run out of blood . . ."

"Yes, maybe so."

The soccer ball soared toward them in an arc. Hanne leaped up and caught it with a smile, then turned to face her colleague.

"Fancy a game?"

An energetic, dismissive gesture extinguished any hope of seeing Håkon Sand play football with the Pakistani boys. Hanne kicked the ball back and groaned. She sat down, rubbing her tender instep.

"Out of practice."

"What do you really think about that case?" Håkon Sand asked.

"Truth to tell, I don't know. Hopefully, it's just nonsense. But there's something or other about it I don't like. Despite everything, the guy must have gone to a lot of bother."

"Or lady."

"I don't honestly believe a woman would do something like that. It's kind of . . . a bit too masculine. All that blood."

"But what if it wasn't a prank? What if those three places were scenes of actual crimes? What if . . . ?"

"Don't you have enough to do, Håkon? Is it necessary to spend time on what-if crimes? In that case, you'll get plenty to keep you busy in the future, that's for sure."

Slightly peeved, she donned her socks and shoes and rolled her trousers down.

"Game over. We need to get back to work," she insisted.

They ambled into the station. Some gilded monstrosity hanging from the ceiling in a feeble attempt at decorating the enormous foyer seemed about to collapse from the heat. The sunshine was reflected so brilliantly it was painful to look at.

No great loss if the whole piece of junk takes a dive, Hanne Wilhelmsen thought.

Then she took the elevator to the second floor.

Håkon's speculations concerning the Saturday night massacres consumed her thoughts, which was immensely annoying.

She now had five rape cases, seven assaults, and a suspected case of incest to work on. It was more than enough. It was true they had a special group to deal with child abuse, but during this absurd spring it seemed that little children were becoming increasingly valuable as sexual objects. They all had to take a share of the load. The case assigned to her was of the kind that would typically be dropped. Clinically, there was no sign of anything untoward. It did not matter that the child had changed character completely, to the total despair of both mother and kindergarten, and a psychologist had established with a great degree of certainty that something or other had happened. Regardless, this was as far distant from securing a conviction as from here to the moon. "Something or other" was not exactly specific, seen from a legal point of view. All the same, it conflicted with her innermost instincts as a police officer not to try a bit harder. During the judicial examination, the youngster had said quite a lot but had gone completely silent when Hanne had carefully tried to coax out the name of the person with "weird pee, like milk." Another judicial review would be her last-ditch effort, but it would have to wait. At least for a couple of weeks.

What if . . .

Hanne Wilhelmsen was sitting with feet on the desk, hands folded behind her head, and eyes half closed.

What if something really had happened in the woodshed in Tøyen, in the workmen's hut beside the River Lo, and in the parking lot at Vaterland? In that case, it was grotesque. The blood couldn't possibly come from a single person. Three or four people meeting their cruel fates in each of these places was so totally improbable that — at least for the moment — she had to exclude the possibility.

She jumped when Chief Inspector Kaldbakken entered the room and jerked her feet off the desk.

"Not enough to do, Wilhelmsen?" he grumbled. "All you need to do is come to me, then you'll have more than enough to keep your hands full!"

"No, thanks all the same."

Despite her boss's stern look and the unflattering situation in which she had just been found, she knew that he knew.

"I've got more than enough. We all have."

Her boss took a seat.

"Have you made any progress with Saturday's rape? That lady student?"

Chief Inspector Kaldbakken must be one

of the last people to call female students ladies. There were rumors he still wore his student cap on May 17 as well.

"No, nothing in particular, just the usual. No one has seen anything, no one has heard anything. She's finding it hugely difficult to give more than a vague description. You've seen the sketch yourself — it looks like anyone and everyone. We've received about fifty tip-offs and Erik has been going through them. None of them seems especially interesting. So he says, at least. I'll have a look through them myself."

"I don't like it." He cleared his throat and then coughed for fully four minutes.

"You should give up smoking, Kaldbakken," she said in a hushed tone, noting it sounded like the second-to-last stage of emphysema. He should stop. Really.

"That's what my wife says too," he replied, half choking, and ended the paroxysm with vigorous hawking, producing a great deal of muck with a revolting consistency. A well-used gigantic handkerchief was raised to his mouth and filled with the stuff. Hanne Wilhelmsen tactfully turned away, letting her eye rest on two sparrows pecking each other on the windowsill. It might be too hot for them too.

"I don't like it," he repeated. "Rapes

93

seldom come singly. Have you heard back from Forensics?"

"No, it's far too early. It usually takes weeks to get anything from them."

"Chase them down, Wilhelmsen. Chase them down. I'm really quite concerned."

With no little effort and strain, he got to his feet, coughing all the way back to his office.

THURSDAY, JUNE 3

It was not easy to take time off, just like that, all of a sudden. Nevertheless, his two colleagues had been extremely understanding and demonstrated goodwill by accommodating his patients at short notice. It was a financial loss. On the other hand, it had been many years since he had treated himself to a proper vacation.

Vacation and vacation. He had a great deal to do. It was still somewhat unclear where he should begin. And so he started with a swim. The baths were surprisingly full, even at this time, seven o'clock in the morning. The chlorine miasma hung densely above the swimmers — it had probably been recently replenished. Some appeared to be regular patrons, greeting each other and chatting at the poolside. Others were more purposeful, swimming to and fro in the fifty-meter-long swimming pool without paying attention to anyone else and without looking at anybody. They just swam, swam, and swam. So did he.

After a hundred meters, he was exhausted. After two hundred, he realized he wasn't hampered only by his years but also by too much body fat. The difficulty began to ease off after another two lengths. He had fallen into a rhythm his heart could accept. His body was far more sluggish than the others splashing steadily past him, up and down, up and down. Their muscular torsos trailed a wake, like heavy vessels in miniature. He hung on to the stern wave of a garish pair of swimming trunks. After seven hundred meters, he felt ready. It was a remarkable start to the day. He could not remember when he'd last had time for swimming. As he hauled himself onto the edge of the pool, he pulled in his abdomen and thrust out his chest. It didn't last farther than the stairway to the changing rooms, where he squeezed the air out through clenched teeth and let his upper body sink back where it belonged.

He found comfort in the sauna. The others did not look quite the same, in heat of almost a hundred degrees, their complexions florid. While he was sitting there, with a towel wrapped self-consciously around his waist, he decided that his first step was visiting the apartment block where his daughter lived. Had lived. He had to do something with that apartment. It was out of the question she should ever move back there. But he wouldn't force her to make a decision yet. They had plenty of time. For the moment.

He felt clean and lighter than his weight of approximately one hundred kilos. It was drizzling outside, but the delicate canopy of cloud was unable to turn down the thermostat. It remained far too warm for the time of year. Even in the middle of July, eighteen degrees Celsius at eight o'clock in the morning would be impressive. At this season it was almost terrifying. Perhaps there was something in all that talk about the ozone layer.

With less difficulty than usual, he got into the car, illegally parked in a disability parking bay. The training session had benefited him. He should do it more often. He needed to sharpen up.

Fourteen minutes later he found a parking space large enough, only fifty meters away from his daughter's address. Looking at his watch again, he realized it was a bit early to disturb anyone. The ones who were going to work would certainly not have time to talk to him. Those who were staying at home were probably not yet up. To kill time, he grabbed a couple of tabloids from a news-stand and stepped into a bakery already tempting busy morning people with the delicious aroma of fresh bread and buns.

After three bread rolls, a quarter liter of milk, and two cups of coffee, it was late enough to make a start. He headed for the car to insert more coins into the parking meter before approaching the building. Fishing out his keys, he let himself into the apartment block. There were two apartments on each floor and five stories in total. It was just as easy to start on the ground.

A homemade porcelain plaque announced that Hans Christiansen and Lena Ødegård lived in the apartment on the left. He stood to attention and peremptorily rang the doorbell. No answer. He tried again, but there was still no sound.

Not a good start. Well, he would just have to return in the afternoon. On the door directly opposite, there was no nameplate at all. At the entrance door, he had noticed that a foreigner lived there. It was impossible for him to ascertain whether it was the name of a woman or a man. Whoever it was obviously hadn't found it necessary to replace the nameplate previously adorning the door — a lighter area was clearly outlined on the wood, with a screw hole at either end.

An audible buzzing sounded inside the apartment when he pressed the doorbell, followed by the patter of footsteps just inside the door. But nothing happened. *Bzzzz.* He tried again. Still no reaction, but he was now convinced there was somebody there. Irritated, he rang one more time, for quite a long period. Discourteously long, he thought, as he rang yet again.

Eventually the door chain rattled, and the door opened a chink. The chain prevented it from opening more than ten centimeters. Inside stood a woman. She was petite, perhaps just over five feet in height. Her clothes were dowdy, cheap, and probably fashioned from one hundred percent synthetic fabrics. They glistened in a glimmer of light radiating from someplace or other. The woman looked terrified.

"You police?"

"No, I'm not from the police," he said, attempting to smile as kindly and encouragingly as possible.

"You not police, you not come in," the little woman said, trying to shut the door.

Quick as a flash, he moved his foot into the tiny opening, just in time to prevent the door from closing completely. He regretted his action when he saw the terror in her eyes.

"Relax," he ventured in desperation. "Take it easy, I just want to speak to you for a moment. I'm Kristine Håverstad's father. The girl on the second floor. Just above here.

"Second floor," he repeated, trying to make her understand. Then he realized he had made a mistake.

"First floor, I mean. My daughter. She lives upstairs."

Perhaps she believed him. Maybe she realized on reflection it was unlikely anyone would come to molest her at half past nine in the morning. Anyway, she withdrew the chain and cautiously opened the door. He looked at her inquiringly, and she motioned for him to come inside.

The apartment was incredibly spartan. It was identical to his daughter's but looked smaller all the same. It must have been because of the lack of furnishings. A settee was placed along one living room wall but was not supplemented by either a coffee table or armchairs, so the room could not really be called a lounge. It clearly also served as a bed, as when he glanced into the bedroom, it was entirely empty, apart from two suitcases sitting in one corner. In the living room, there was also a small din-

100

ing table with a straight-backed chair. On the wall opposite the settee, an old television, evidently a black-and-white set, sat on a side table. The floors were bare, as were the walls. Apart from a large unframed color photograph of an aristocratic man with an aquiline nose and a highly decorated uniform — he immediately recognized the former Shah of Persia.

"Are you from Iran?" he asked, happy to have hit upon something to open the conversation.

"Iran! Yes!"

The tiny woman smiled submissively.

"I from Iran. Yes."

"Do you speak Norwegian, or would you prefer to speak English?" he continued, wondering if he could sit down. He decided to remain standing. If he was to sit, then she would either have to remain standing, or else sit beside him on the sofa. Which she would probably find unpleasant.

"I understand Norwegian fine," she replied. "Not speak so well, maybe."

"I think you manage very well," he encouraged her. It was becoming uncomfortable to stand, so he changed his mind. He seized hold of the dining chair, dragged it over to the settee, and asked if it was in order to use it.

"Just sit, sit down," she said, obviously now more relaxed. She sat at the farthest edge of the sofa.

"As I said," he began, clearing his throat. "I'm Kristine's father. Kristine Håverstad. The young woman on the floor above. Perhaps you've heard what happened to her last Saturday."

It was difficult to talk about it. Especially to a little foreign woman from Iran he had never met before and probably would never see again. He cleared his throat again.

"I'm just making a few inquiries on my own. For my own sake, so to speak. You've probably already spoken to the police."

The woman nodded.

"Were you here when it happened?"

Her hesitation was obvious, and he didn't entirely understand why she decided to trust him. Perhaps she didn't understand it herself either.

"No, I not here that night. I in Denmark that weekend. Last weekend. With friends. But I not say that to lady from police. I say I sleeping."

"Okay. You've got friends in Denmark."

"No. Not friend in Denmark. Not friend in Norway. But some friend in Germany. They I meet in Copinghagen. Not seen them in long, long, long time. I back here

Sunday late."

The woman wasn't beautiful, but she had a strong, genial face. Her skin was much lighter than other Iranians he had seen. In a sense she was dark, but her hair was not jet-black, though neither was it dark brown. It was more what his wife in the old days had called "local color," but nevertheless it was thick and lustrous. And she even had blue eyes!

With a little assistance from gestures and English, she related her sad story. She was an asylum seeker and had been waiting for thirteen slow, bureaucratic months to have her application for sanctuary in the Kingdom of Norway processed. Her family, what little was left of it, was scattered to the winds. Her mother had died of natural causes three years previously, many years after her husband had escaped to Norway. He had been a lawyer in the Shah's Iran, and the family had led a favored existence. They were poorly rewarded when the regime fell. Two of her brothers were killed in the prisons of the Ayatollah. She and her sister had managed all right until a year and a half ago. A fellow member of their cell had been captured, and after three days and nights of torture had been broken. The next day he was killed. And the day after that, soldiers stood at their door.

She had already been tipped off and traveled across the border to Turkey with help from fellow partisans with better cover than she had. From Turkey she had flown to Norway and what she thought would be a life with her father. On arrival at the airport, the immigration police had informed her that her father had died of a heart attack three days earlier. An attorney assigned to her as soon as she was placed in Tanum Reception Center in Bærum had quickly discovered that she was the legal heir of her father's small estate, comprising a fully paid apartment, five beautiful Persian rugs, a few articles of furniture, and a bank account containing forty thousand kroner. She had sold the rugs and furniture, netting more than a hundred thousand kroner, money she had sent to Iran, hoping her sister could derive some benefit from it. She had received no reply, something not entirely unexpected. She could only hope for the best. The forty thousand in the bank account covered her own subsistence. In that way, she would not be a burden on Norwegian society.

"I lucky. Not need live in Tanum. Live here. More good that, for me."

Her trip to Denmark had been illegal in

the sense that, as an asylum seeker with no passport, she could not leave the country. However, with her atypical appearance, she was able to pass as Scandinavian to over-worked customs officers. It had been un-problematic. But it also meant she could not provide him with any information he was actually looking for.

He stood up.

"Well, thanks for the chat. Good luck for the future."

In the doorway, he paused and extended his hand. "I hope the police are decent to you."

He couldn't be certain, but he had an idea that a worried look flitted across her face.

"I mean, I hope you are allowed to stay here in the country," he said more precisely.

"I hope too," she replied.

He was on his way upstairs when the door slammed shut. The rattling of the door chain as it was replaced followed him all the way to the next floor. He stood for a moment on the landing, with a peculiar feeling that something had escaped him. A few seconds later, he shook it off and rang the doorbell of the next apartment.

Four days had passed since the dreadful rape in Homansbyen, and she was not a single step closer to a solution. On the contrary. Detective Inspector Hanne Wilhelmsen had frighteningly little to report on her work in connection with the case. The scale of her frustration was absolute, unaccustomedly so.

But what should she do? Most of the previous day had been spent interviewing witnesses in two of the assault cases. They were overdue, and angry lawyers' letters chasing these offenses were shrieking at her from the top of her pile of case documents. She still had to conduct at least five interviews in one case, the most serious a knifing drama in which the knife had swept past the main artery in the victim's thigh by only millimeters. When she would find the time for five outstanding witness interviews was something of a conundrum.

The incest case was hanging over her like an unpaid bill, with the deadline long expired. The night before, she had been awakened by a bad conscience and terrible dreams. She had arranged to have the new judicial review earlier than originally planned. It would take a whole day. First there would be a home visit and a "getting-to-know-you" round. There would then be lemonade in the canteen and a drive in a police car and a "trust-the-police" round.

She didn't have a whole day. She didn't have even half a day.

The piles of documents facing her were making her feel sick. If the inhabitants of the city had any idea how helpless the police were currently, as they staggered through the crime wave, barely able to keep their heads above water, there would be such an outcry they would be granted an extra hundred million kroner and fifty new posts on the spot. Currently, the police's ability to keep criminality at bay was an illusion, pure and simple. This would be the right time to commit a major crime, Hanne Wilhelmsen surmised. Ninety-nine percent chance of not being caught.

She should not have had that thought.

The robbery alarm sounded. The intercom system was linked up, and the superintendent's deep monotone voice reached everyone in the department. Nor Savings Bank in Sagene had been raided. Everyone had to assemble in the conference room. Quick as lightning, she donned her motorbike helmet and leather jacket.

She just missed getting away with it. Only a meter and a half from the door to freedom at the top of the staircase leading to the personnel entrance, she was grabbed by the collar. The superintendent laughed when she turned around, shamefaced.

"Don't try to kid a kidder," he said. "Get yourself to the meeting room."

"No, honestly," she ventured. "I need to go out. Anyway, I've so much on my plate just now I can't contribute anything at all. Really. Honestly. I simply can't take on anything more."

Possibly it was something in her tone of voice. Probably it was of some importance that she was decidedly his best detective. Or maybe it was her unusually tired facial expression, with obvious dark circles below her eyes and an unbecoming sharpness in her profile. Whatever it was, the superintendent stood for a moment, evidently uncertain.

"Okay, then," he said finally. "Off you go. But don't make it a habit."

Infinitely relieved, she headed for the door. What she was going to do, she had no idea. She just had to get out.

One thing was just as good as another. It was impossible to visit a crime scene too many times. Anyhow, it would give her a sense of doing something specific.

They bumped into each other in the doorway. She was fishing out the keys from the pocket of her leather jacket when he came barging out. Hanne Wilhelmsen had to take a step back to avoid falling over. The enormous man was equally jolted. He apologized profusely, at length, before recognizing her.

The dentist was too old to blush. Moreover, his skin was coarse and unshaven, which would hardly allow any redness to show through. Nevertheless, Hanne Wilhelmsen noticed a slight twitch in his eyes as he hastily explained that he had been visiting his daughter's apartment to collect something. He suddenly realized he was not carrying anything.

"Unfortunately, it wasn't there," he said by way of excuse. "She must have been mistaken."

Detective Inspector Hanne Wilhelmsen said nothing. The awkward silence was in her favor. He knew that, as he coughed abruptly, looking at his watch and adding that he was late for an important meeting.

"Could you come for a brief interview with me at eight o'clock tomorrow morning?" she asked, without giving him the opportunity to slip past her.

He considered for a fleeting moment.

"Tomorrow morning? Um, that would be a bit difficult, I think. It's so busy right now."

"It's quite important. We'll meet at eight

o'clock, okay?"

It was clear he felt extremely uneasy.

"Well, all right, eight o'clock then. Perhaps a few minutes past?"

"That's absolutely fine." She smiled. "A few minutes before or after won't matter at all."

Then she let him by. She remained standing there, following him with her eyes until he was sitting in his car some distance away. She went upstairs to her old friend on the first floor, where she received another overwhelming welcome and the expected confirmation that a very pleasant man, the poor girl's father, had been there and struck up a cozy conversation.

Hanne Wilhelmsen did not listen carefully to what the old man was saying. Barely a quarter of an hour and half a cup of coffee later, she thanked him and left. Knitting her brow, she sat for a while astride the Harley without starting the engine. For one reason or another, the meeting with the father of the young girl who had been raped made her feel she was participating in some kind of race. A race she did not care for in the slightest.

It was unfortunate to be caught so obviously red-handed. He regretted having been so unprepared for his meeting with the policewoman. The danger of bumping into the police was obvious, but all the same, he had not taken it into consideration. It would also cost him an embarrassing interview tomorrow. Well, he would just have to tough it out.

In the afternoon, he had been back to the apartment block, and now there was only one man on the fourth floor and a young woman on the second he had not quizzed. It did not matter, since the other neighbors were able to tell him that the man on the fourth floor had been abroad for two months, and the young woman had been staying at her parents' the previous weekend.

The old man was the only one who had told him anything specific. About a red car. A bright red foreign car that had been parked thirty meters away across the street from around eleven o'clock on Saturday evening until break of dawn on Sunday morning.

Did the police know about the red car? Was it of any real interest? It might belong to anyone at all. It was highly unlikely an attacker would have his car parked in the vicinity of the crime scene while the attack was being executed. On the other hand, the heavily built dentist was far from inclined to assign rapists to the same category as other lawbreakers. His understanding of sexual offenders was along the lines of slavering, primitive creatures of inferior intelligence. Although he knew better, and had modified his opinion somewhat now that he was pursuing one himself, he could not — would not — preclude the possibility that the guy might be the owner of the red car.

In any case, it was all he had. A red car. A sedan. Unknown type, unknown registration number.

He sighed stoically and busied himself making some dinner for himself and his silent daughter.

It was nearing ten o'clock in the evening, and they were lying on the floor, having made love. They had two quilts underneath them, and over them a cool early summer breeze from the balcony door, which, audaciously enough, was left ajar. The curtains were drawn defensively, and they had kept as quiet as possible. From the other balcony doors they could hear distant noises: a married couple quarreling on the floor below and a noisy television film from the next-door neighbor. Hanne and Cecilie had been lying there since before the evening news.

"Why are we lying here really?" Hanne giggled. "It's a bit hard. I've got a pain in my tailbone."

"What a wimp! Look at me, I've got burns!"

Cecilie bent her knee and drew it level with her face. It was true. She had a burn, quite a sizable one at that. They never learned. It had happened several times previously, one of them ending up with nasty marks on elbows or knees from friction against the carpet as soon as they landed outside the quilt beneath them.

"Poor you," Hanne said, kissing the sore knee. "Why do we keep lying here?"

"Because it's so fantastically comfortable," her beloved explained, sitting up.

"Are you going away?"

"No, I just want one of the quilts. I'm freezing."

She grabbed hold of the top quilt and pulled. Which meant Hanne was rolled around onto her stomach. Kneeling, Cecilie kissed her exactly where her back divided.

"Poor tailbone," she said, snuggling down beside Hanne and spreading the quilt over them both. Hanne turned on her side, supporting her head with her elbow, and stroking a forefinger slowly across her partner's right breast.

"What would you do if someone raped me?" she asked suddenly.

"Raped you? Why would anybody rape you? You're not careless enough to get raped."

"Honestly, darling. You really must give that up. It has nothing to do with being careless when a girl gets raped."

"Oh, no? Why have none of our friends been raped, then? Why are there continual reports in the newspapers about girls raped in the most suspect places in the city, at the most peculiar times? If you're careful, you won't get raped."

Hanne Wilhelmsen was not ready for an argument, though her partner's lack of insight irritated her. She felt much too happy to quarrel. She definitely did not want to. Instead she leaned forward, letting her tongue glide in wet circles around Cecilie's areola, painstakingly, so as not to touch the actual nipple. Suddenly she stopped.

"Seriously," she insisted. "What would you do? How would you feel?"

The other woman sat up slowly, supporting herself with her arms. She half turned to face her. A green light from the display on the gigantic stereo system made her

114

features almost ethereal.

"Now you look like the most beautiful ghost in the world," Hanne said softly, laughing. "The world's absolutely most beautiful ghost."

She snatched at a lock of her long pale blonde hair and curled it several times around her finger.

"Please," she asked once more. "Can't you say what you would do?"

Finally Cecilie realized she was serious. She straightened her back ever so slightly, as though it would help her ability to think. Then she said, loud and clear, and with great seriousness: "I would kill the guy."

She stopped abruptly, considering for a further ten seconds.

"Yep, I would most certainly murder him."

It was precisely the response Hanne wanted. She sat up too and kissed her partner tenderly.

"Right answer." She smiled. "Now we must sleep."

Friday, June 4

Finn Håverstad rarely ventured into the east end of the city. His dental practice was situated in a villa in the Frogner district: enormous, old, and expensive of upkeep, so no one could afford to live there. The ground floor accommodated a firm of architects, one of the few that had managed to survive the lengthy financial crisis in the profession. On the first floor, three dentists had their exam rooms in bright, attractive premises flooded with sunshine and fresh air.

His residence was situated in Volvat. Centrally located but at the same time rural, on a site measuring around half an acre. Although the dental practice had been extremely profitable during the last fifteen years, it began with the good fortune of receiving an advance on his inheritance that had placed him in a position to buy the property in 1978. His daughter had loved the house. He could walk to his work in twenty minutes — something, all the same, he never actually did.

It smelled different on the other side of the city. Not exactly dirtier, perhaps not meaner either, but . . . it had a stronger smell. Exhaust fumes lay thicker, and the city had a more pungent odor, as though it had forgotten to put on deodorant in just this spot. Moreover, the level of noise here was far louder. He did not feel comfortable.

It was typically Norwegian to situate police headquarters in the most deplorable district of the city. The state had probably bought the site for next to nothing. Parking provision was dreadful too. He drove his BMW gingerly into an empty gap at the foot of the long incline leading up to the actual building. He had to wait for ten minutes before there was a parking space. A youth slammed aggressively out of an opening in an old Amazon, grazing the corner of the wall on the bend as he turned out of the garage building. A heavily scraped yellow-and-black patch on the wall indicated the boy was not the first to do so. Paying due attention to the danger, the dentist eased his car into place and left it reluctantly when he saw he was already a quarter of an hour behind schedule.

She didn't mention he was eighteen minutes late. On the whole, she appeared cheerful and accommodating, in fact downright pleasant. He started to feel extremely insecure.

"It won't take long," she said reassuringly. "Coffee? Or maybe tea?"

Hanne Wilhelmsen fetched coffee for both of them and lit a cigarette for herself after his assurance it did not inconvenience him in the least.

For a frighteningly long period of time, she remained sitting, blowing cigarette smoke into the room, following the exhalation with a lingering look and keeping totally silent. He moved restlessly in his chair, partly because he found it uncomfortable. In the end he could no longer endure the silence.

"Is there anything in particular you wanted from me?" he said, feeling surprised at how submissive he sounded.

The detective inspector suddenly stared at him, as though she hadn't known until now that he was sitting there.

"Oh, yes," she replied, almost jauntily, "there is something in particular I wanted of you. First . . ."

Looking at him with a quizzical expression, she stubbed out her cigarette and, obviously receiving the answer she was looking for when he gesticulated with one arm, immediately lit another.

"I really ought to give it up," she said confidingly. "I've a boss here who has smoked like this for thirty years. You should hear him cough! Shush!"

Her posture stiffened as she tilted her head. Far down the corridor they could hear a rattling fit of coughing.

"There you hear it," she said triumphantly. "This stuff is really dangerous!"

Gazing disapprovingly at the half-full pack of twenty, she fell into something of a reverie.

"And so there are the two of us, then," she said abruptly, so loudly he jumped in his seat. Noticing that he had begun to sweat, he stroked his upper lip as discreetly as possible with his index finger.

"First the formalities," she said indifferently, hammering down his name, address, and date of birth as quickly as he stated them. "Next I have to warn you about the following matters: you must tell the police the truth; it is a punishable offense to make a false declaration to the police; you are in fact a witness . . ."

She smiled, and their eyes met again.

". . . and not the accused in a criminal

case. They can actually lie as much as they want! Unfair, really, don't you think?"

The large head nodded up and down. At that very moment, he would have agreed with this woman about anything at all. She was scarier than she appeared. The first time he met her, the previous Monday, he had noticed in passing she was attractive. Quite tall and slim but with generous hips and full breasts. Now she seemed more like an Amazon. He stroked his finger under his nose once more, but it did not help. Digging out a freshly ironed pocket handkerchief, he wiped both his temples.

"Are you feeling hot in here? I apologize. This building is completely unsuitable for the kind of temperatures we're experiencing just now."

She didn't make any move to open the window.

"However," she said instead, "you have no need to give evidence. You can refuse. But I don't suppose you'll do that?"

He shook his head so vehemently he had a feeling the drops of sweat were splashing.

"That's fine," she established. "We'll make a start."

For fully half an hour, the detective inspector posed completely unthreatening questions. When he had arrived at his daughter's apartment last Sunday. Where she had been sitting at that time, quite precisely. Whether she had been wearing any clothes. Whether there were any items there he might have disposed of. Whether he had noticed anything unusual apart from his daughter's condition — smells, sounds, or anything of that nature. About how his daughter was now, reactions she had experienced in the days that followed. How he himself was feeling.

Although it hurt him deeply to talk about the case, he began to feel relieved. His shoulders sank a little, and the room appeared somewhat less uncomfortable. He even drank some of the coffee while she took a break in the interview to write all of it down on the antiquated golf ball typewriter on her desk.

"Not especially up to date, that there," he said tentatively.

Without pausing and without looking at him, she told him she was waiting her turn to be allocated her own computer. Perhaps next week. Maybe in a month's time.

Twenty minutes later she was finished and lit herself another cigarette.

"What were you doing at Kristine's neighbors' yesterday?"

It was inconceivable the question should

catch him so completely unawares. He had known, of course, that it would come. In a flash he considered the consequences of lying. A fifty-year-old life on the mainly law-abiding side of society gained the upper hand.

"I wanted to carry out some investigations of my own," he admitted.

There. Now he had said it. He had not lied. It felt good. He saw she realized he had weighed up whether or not to concoct a story.

"Are you playing private detective, then?"

It was not sarcastic. She had in effect changed character. Her facial expression softened, she turned her chair to face him and held eye contact with him for quite a spell, for the first time since his arrival.

"Listen to me, Håverstad. I don't know how you're feeling, of course. But I can imagine. To some extent, at least. I have dealt with forty-two rape cases. No one gets used to them. None of them are alike. Apart from one thing — they are equally horrendous. Both for the victims and for the people who love them. I have seen it lots of times."

Now she stood up and opened the window. She placed a small, ugly brown glass ashtray in the gap to prevent it from closing again.

"I have often . . . Believe me! . . . It has often crossed my mind what my reaction would be if my . . ."

She checked herself.

". . . if one of my nearest and dearest had been exposed to something like this. It can only be speculation, of course, as I am in the fortunate situation never to have experienced such a thing."

Her slender hand made a fist, punching three times on the desktop.

"But I believe I would be bursting with thoughts of revenge. First I would truly make an effort to show kindness and consideration. A great deal of despair can be channeled into giving others care and support. You don't need to tell me, though, you don't succeed. I know that. Rape victims are difficult to reach. And then it's easy to be consumed by thoughts of vengeance. Revenge . . ."

Crossing her arms over her chest, she stared at a distant point above his head.

"I think we underestimate our need for revenge. You should hear the lawyers! If you merely hint at revenge as an aspect of punishment, they come out with lectures on legal history, saying we left that behind

123

many centuries ago. Revenge is not reckoned to be honorable enough here in the north. It's demeaning, it's contemptible, and perhaps most of all . . ."

Biting her lip, she searched for a word.

". . . primitive! We regard it as primitive! A hugely mistaken concept, if you ask me. The need for revenge is deeply rooted in us. The frustration people feel when sex offenders receive six months in jail naturally can't be mitigated by legal phrases about universal prevention and considerations of rehabilitation. People want revenge! A person who has behaved hellishly should have a hellish time himself. And that's that."

Finn Håverstad had some idea where this odd detective inspector was going. He was still plagued by insecurity, but there was something in her sense of commitment, in her eyes, in the gestures she was making with her entire body to emphasize her points, that made him feel this woman would never do him any harm. This was her method of cautioning him against what he had already embarked upon. A warning, quite clearly, but a well-meaning and compassionate one.

"But you know, Håverstad, that's not how it operates here with us. It's not the way to go about it, having people solve crimes on their own, taking revenge at dead of night, to the secret rejoicing of the public. That only happens in films. And perhaps in America."

There was a knock at the door. A bizarre figure flung it open without waiting for an answer. At least six and a half feet tall, he had a closely shaven head, an unkempt red beard, and an inverted cross on his earlobe.

"Oh, excuse me," he blurted out at the sight of Håverstad, without seeming altogether sincere. He looked at the detective inspector.

"Friday beer at four o'clock, are you coming?"

"If I'm allowed to make it not only a Friday beer but a Friday Munkholm, then fine!"

"We'll say four o'clock, then," the giant replied, slamming the door behind him.

"He's a policeman," she assured him apologetically. "An undercover detective. They sometimes look a bit strange."

The atmosphere had changed. The lecture was over. She placed the two typewritten sheets in front of him to read through. It was quickly accomplished. They contained nothing concerning the topic they had been talking about — what she had been talking about — for the past half hour. The detec-

125

tive inspector pointed with her forefinger at the foot of the second sheet, and he signed.

"Also here," she added, indicating the margin of the first page.

It was obvious he could leave. He got to his feet, but she waved away his hand, extended to shake hers in farewell.

"I'll come out with you."

Locking the office door behind her, she walked at his side down a passageway with blue doors and flooring. People were scurrying to and fro in the corridor, none wearing uniforms. They both stopped at the stairs leading to the exit. Now she was willing to shake hands.

"Take my good advice, Håverstad. Don't stick your nose into something you might not be able to smell. Do something else. Take your daughter away on a vacation. Go on a trip to the mountains. Travel to the south. Whatever. But let us get on with our job. On our own."

He mumbled a few parting words before descending the stairs. Hanne Wilhelmsen followed him with her gaze until he approached the massive metal doors holding the unbearable temperature inside. She took a few paces toward the windows facing west, reaching them at exactly the same time as he came into sight below. His trudging figure and rolling gait almost made him look like an old man. He stood still for a moment, straightening his back, before vanishing downstairs to the underground parking lot.

Detective Inspector Hanne Wilhelmsen felt great pity for the man.

Kristine Håverstad normally took pleasure in being at home on her own. Now she was incapable of enjoying anything at all. When her father rose, she was awake, but she'd stayed in bed until she heard the door slam behind him around half past seven. After that, she had used up all the hot water. First she showered for twenty minutes, scrubbing herself red and sore, and then she had taken a long, boiling-hot bubble bath. This had become her routine, practically a ritual, every morning.

Now she was sitting, wearing an old jogging suit and a pair of well-worn sealskin slippers, sifting through her CD collection. When she had left home two years earlier, she had taken only the most recent ones with her, and her favorites. The pile she had left behind was fairly extensive. She grabbed an old a-ha CD, *Hunting High and Low*. The title was apposite. She felt she was searching for something she had no idea where to find. She did not have any idea even of what it was. As she was opening the case, she dropped it on the floor. One of the hinges broke, and she cursed softly when the two sides separated and could not be fixed together again. Angrily, she attempted to manage what she knew was impossible, resulting in the other hinge breaking too. Furious, she threw both pieces onto the floor and began to cry. Damn CD producers! She wept for half an hour.

Morten Harket had not broken in two. Leaning forward, with stiff, muscular arms, he was staring at a place somewhere to the right of her with an inscrutable black-and-white gaze. Kristine Håverstad had studied medicine for four years. She knew her anatomy. She fished the little cover photograph from the plastic fragments in front of her. That muscle she could see was not visible in normal people. It required exercise, a great deal of working out. She felt her own slim upper arms. The triceps was there, of course, but not visible. It certainly was on Morten Harket. The underside of his upper arm bulged powerfully and distinctly. She sat staring.

The man had been very fit. His triceps muscles had been conspicuous. When she tried to think back to that dreadful night, it was impossible to understand when she had caught sight of it. Perhaps she hadn't. Perhaps she had simply felt it. But she was one hundred percent certain. Her rapist had possessed bulging triceps.

A fact. That she did not know what to do with.

Noises suddenly were audible from the hallway, and she jumped as though she were caught red-handed committing a crime of which she was oblivious. Adrenaline pumping through her bloodstream, she retrieved the pieces of broken plastic as quick as lightning, endeavoring to hide them in the enormous heap of unbroken disks facing her. Then she started to cry again.

Everything terrified her at the moment. This morning, a tiny bird had flown toward the huge panorama window in the living room, while she was sitting there trying to force down some food. The sound made her leap skyward. She knew exactly what it was; it was quite common for the poor things to smack into the window. They virtually always came to no harm. Occasionally they remained lying there for half an hour or so before wobbling to their feet, flapping their wings gingerly a few times, and flying dizzily into the air again. This time as she had stepped outside to pick up the little bird, feeling its tiny heart beating time and time again, she felt deeply distressed. In the end the bird had died. Probably of shock because she had lifted it. She felt guilty and ashamed.

Her father leaned over her. He pulled her to her feet, and she staggered, as though she were physically incapable of supporting her slight frame in a standing position. He could not recall her being so thin and was startled when he grasped her skinny wrists to prevent her from toppling over. He carefully hauled her across to the settee, where she allowed herself to be placed on the deep cushions without any protest. He sat down beside her, leaving a narrow space between them. Then he changed his mind, moving slightly closer, but stopping short when she made a move to pull herself back. Solicitously, he clasped her hand, and she let him hold it.

There was no other physical contact between them. Kristine was glad of that. She couldn't manage to pull herself together, though she really wanted to do so. She wanted at least to say something, to say anything at all.

"I'm so sorry, Dad. So terribly sorry."

In fact he didn't hear what she was saying. She spoke softly and moreover was crying so heartbrokenly that half her words were not properly enunciated. But at least she was talking. For a moment he was unsure whether he should say something in reply. Would she regard his silence as a sign of helplessness? Or was it exactly the best thing, not to say anything, only to listen? As a compromise, he coughed.

That was obviously the right thing to do. She drifted toward him, slowly, almost hesitantly, but eventually her face was close to his neck. That was where she stayed. He sat like a pillar of salt, with one arm around her and the other hand in hers. He was not sitting comfortably, but he didn't move a muscle for half an hour. There and then he knew the decision he had made when he found his daughter on the floor less than a week earlier, devastated and destroyed, a decision he had doubted as recently as his visit to the police that morning, had been correct after all.

"Is it possible to make any sense at all of this?"

Since they had so many major cases, no one had a monopoly on the so-called operations room. It was not much to boast about anyway, but was at least a room, just as good as any other.

Erik Henriksen was sweaty and redder in the face than usual, making him look like a walking traffic light. Right now he was seated. On a tilted worktable facing him lay a sea of report sheets. These were the tip-offs in the Kristine Håverstad case.

The officer looked up at Hanne Wilhelmsen.

"There's a lot of peculiar stuff here." He laughed. "Listen to this. 'The sketch bears a striking resemblance to Arne Høgtveit, the municipal court judge. Regards from Ulf of Nordland.' "

Hanne Wilhelmsen smiled broadly. Ulf of Nordland was a notorious criminal who found himself inside prison walls more often than outside. Judge Høgtveit had probably seen to his most recent stay.

"Actually, that's not so idiotic. It does look a bit like him," she said, crumpling the report and aiming for the wastepaper bin beside the door. She scored a hit.

"Or this one," Erik Henriksen continued. " 'The culprit must be my son. He has been possessed by evil spirits since 1991. He has closed his door to the Lord.' "

"That's not so idiotic either, you know," Hanne Wilhelmsen said. "Have you investigated further?"

"Yes. The man is a clergyman in Drammen. His mother has been a psychiatric patient at Lier Hospital since 1991."

Now she laughed out loud.

"Are they all just like that?"

She scanned the reports that were spread out, seemingly chaotic but probably according to some kind of system.

"That one . . ."

Henriksen clapped the bundle farthest to the left with his hand.

". . . is simply stuff and nonsense."

Unfortunately, that was the largest stack.

"This one . . ."

His fist punched the closer bundle, which was smaller.

". . . is lawyers, judges, and police officers."

Then he let his fingers stray across the table.

"Here are previous sex offenders, here are the usual, men unknown to us, here are people who clearly are too old, and here . . ."

He picked up a slim bundle containing four or five sheets.

". . . these are women."

"Women." Hanne chortled. "Have we received reports about women?"

"Yes. Should I throw them out?"

"You can safely do that. As a matter of form, hold on to the lawyer and police bundle, and perhaps the crazy pile too. But don't waste any time on them. At the moment. Concentrate on the sexual deviants and the usual men without police records. If the reports have been made by people who seem reasonably serious, at least. How many does that leave then?"

He counted quickly. "Twenty-seven men."

"Who have probably not committed the crime." Hanne Wilhelmsen sighed. "But bring them in. As quickly as possible. Let me know if anyone seems particularly interesting. Does that phone work?"

Taken aback, he responded that he assumed so. He lifted the receiver and held it tentatively to his ear for a second.

"Dial tone, anyway. Were you not expecting it to be working?"

"There's always some issue with the equipment in here. Nothing but castoffs no one else wants."

Pulling a slip of paper from her tight jeans, she dialed an Oslo number.

"Senior Technician Bente Reistadvik, please," she requested. Before long the technician was on the line.

"Wilhelmsen, Homicide, Oslo Police, here. I have a couple of cases with you. Firstly . . ."

She glanced again at the note.

"Case number 93-03541. Offense against Kristine Håverstad. We have asked for DNA and also sent over some fibers, hairs, and various fragments."

There was silence for a while, and the detective inspector stared into space without making any notes.

"No, I see. When will it be ready, approximately? As long as that?"

Sighing, she turned around, leaning her posterior on the edge of the desk.

"What about these Saturday night massacres of ours? Have you anything for me on them?"

Ten seconds later she was staring at the red-haired policeman with a startled expression.

"Is that right? Okay."

A pause.

"Exactly."

A lengthy pause. She turned around again, obviously searching for something to write on, and received pen and paper from her colleague. Pulling the telephone cable around the edge of the desk with her, she sat down at the other side of the two desks, which had been placed together.

"Interesting. When can I have that in writing?"

Another pause.

"Great stuff. Thanks very much!"

The receiver banged into place. Hanne Wilhelmsen continued to make notes for a minute and a half. She stared at what she had written for a few moments, without uttering a word. Then, folding the sheet of paper twice, she stood up, placed the note in her back pocket, and left the room without even a word of farewell.

Erik Henriksen sat back, feeling somewhat cheated.

His golden tan was as simulated as his muscle tone. The former was a result of solarium rays, enough to inflict terminal skin cancer on a large group. The bulging muscles had been assisted by artificial substances, more specifically various types of testosterone, mainly anabolic steroids.

He was in love with his own appearance. He was a man. He had always wanted to look like this, especially when he was going through puberty as a skinny, cross-eyed boy on the receiving end of daily thrashings from other boys. His mother had not been able to prevent any of it. With breath reeking of mints and alcohol, she had tried despondently to comfort him when he arrived home with black eyes, scraped knees, and burst lips. However, she stayed hidden behind the curtains rather than intervening when the hooligans in the neighborhood challenged both her and her boy by staging fights ever closer to the apartment block where he lived. He was aware of it, because when he had initially shouted up for help to the kitchen curtains on the first floor, he had seen the movement as she withdrew from the window. She always drew back. What she did not know was that the beatings were caused more by her than by his own puny appearance.

The lads in the street had proper mothers. The kind of cheerful, clever women who offered slices of bread with milk, some of them working, but none of them full-time. The others had annoying, sweet little siblings and, what's more, fathers. Not all of them lived there; at the beginning of the seventies, the trend toward divorce had even reached the small town where he grew up. But the daddies turned up all the same, in cars on Saturday mornings, with sleeves rolled up, beaming smiles, and fishing rods in the trunk of the car. All except his.

The boys called his mother Alkie-Guri. When he was little, really little, he had thought his mother had such a lovely name. Guri. After Alkie-Guri was mentioned, he hated it. From that day to this, he couldn't stand women with that name. He couldn't stand women much in any case.

He survived puberty, barely, and the bullying diminished. He was seventeen and had grown eighteen centimeters in eighteen months. He did not have acne, and his shoulders had broadened. The squint had been repaired in an operation following which he had been required to go about with a humiliating patch over his eye for six months, not exactly increasing his popularity. His hair was blond, and his mother told him he was handsome. For the life of him he could not understand why Aksel, for example, had a girlfriend when no one would even look at him. Aksel was a slightly overweight, bespectacled classmate who, on top of everything else, was at least a head shorter than him.

They weren't actually nasty but simply avoided him and occasionally threw sarcastic comments in his direction. Especially the ladies.

When the boy was in his second year of senior high school, Alkie-Guri lost her marbles completely. She was committed to a psychiatric hospital. He had visited her once, shortly after her incarceration. She was lying in bed then, festooned with pipes and tubes, with her head in the clouds. He had not known what he should do, what he should say. While he was sitting there, in silence, listening to her nonsense, the quilt had slid halfway off her body. Her nightdress was open at the front, and one breast, a skinny, empty sack of flesh with a dark, almost black nipple, had grimaced at him, like a staring, accusing eyeball. Then he left. Since that time, he had never seen his mother. That day he made up his mind about what he would become. No one would be able to torment him again.

Now he was sitting facing a computer screen, pondering deeply. The choice was not entirely easy. He had to restrict himself to the ones who were absolutely sure things. The ones who had nobody. The ones nobody would miss. Now and again he stood up and stepped over to a filing cabinet, taking out files and looking again at the little passport photograph fastened with a paper clip at the top of the first page. The passport photographs always lied, he knew that from bitter experience. However, they conveyed some inkling.

Eventually he was satisfied. He felt his excitement escalate, a real kick, as good as when he measured his muscles and realized he could expect an increase of at least one centimeter on his upper arms, compared with the last measurement.

It was an ingenious arrangement. And most ingenious of all was that he was fooling the others. Fooling and tormenting them. He knew exactly how things stood with them, the idiots in the Criminal Investigation Department at police headquarters. They were utterly bamboozled by these Saturday night massacres. He even knew that's what they were calling them: Saturday night massacres. He smiled. They didn't even have the brains to decipher the clue he had left them. Cretins, all of them.

He rejoiced.

"Tell me, where are you hanging out these days?" Hanne Wilhelmsen asked, collapsing onto the visitor's chair in Håkon Sand's office. He was struggling with a quid of chewing tobacco that was leaking rather too much, and his upper lip formed into a peculiar convex shape as a safeguard against the undoubtedly bitter taste.

"I hardly get a glimpse of you, you know!"

"Court," he mumbled, endeavoring to help the chewing tobacco back into place with his tongue. Having to give up, he stuck his index finger under his lip and pulled out the entire splodge. He shook his finger on the edge of the wastepaper basket, and wiped the remainder on his trousers.

"Pig," Hanne Wilhelmsen muttered.

"I've got a hell of a lot of pressure at the moment, you see," he said, disregarding the comment. "First of all, I'm in court just about every day. Secondly, I have to take my turn with other cases far too often, since people take an excessive amount of sick leave. I'm inundated."

He pointed to one of the customary piles of green that polluted everyone's existence at present.

"I haven't even had a chance to look at them yet! Not so much as a glimpse!"

Leaning forward, Hanne Wilhelmsen opened a folder she had brought with her, setting it down in front of him. She drew her chair up to the desk, so they were sitting there like two friendly first-year pupils sharing a reading book.

"Here you'll at least get to see something exciting. The Saturday night massacres. I've just spoken to Forensics. They aren't finished yet, but the preliminary results are quite interesting. Look at this."

She produced a rigid file with photographs attached, two on each page. There were three sheets, six photos in total. Small white arrows were affixed in two or three places on each photograph, taken from different

141

angles. It was quite difficult to keep the folder open, as its stiffness and inflexibility were causing it to close continually. Lifting it up, she ripped the pages apart. That helped.

"This is from the first one. The woodshed at Tøyen. I requested three samples, taken from different places."

What was the point of that? Håkon Sand wondered but said nothing.

"It turned out to be a damn good idea," Hanne Wilhelmsen commented, reading his thoughts.

"Because here . . ."

She indicated the first picture, where there were only two arrows mounted.

"Here, it was human blood. From a woman. I've asked for a full analysis, but that'll take some time.

"But here . . ." she continued, pointing to the second arrow, then leafing through to the next page and pointing at yet another arrow, on a picture containing three of the little indicators.

"Here we have something different, you understand. Animal blood!"

"Animal blood?"

"Yes. Probably from a pig, but we don't know yet. We'll find out soon."

The sample of human blood had been

taken from approximately the middle of the bloodbath. The animal blood had been situated on the periphery.

She folded up the file but remained sitting beside him without any hint of moving. They said not a word. Hanne noticed he smelled good, a faint scent of aftershave she did not recognize. Neither of them had any idea what the blood sample results might mean.

"If all the blood had come from an animal, the prankster theory would have been considerably reinforced," Hanne mumbled after a while, more to herself than to Håkon. "But now it turns out it's not only from an animal . . ."

Glancing at the clock, she jumped.

"I must dash. Friday beer with my old buddies. Have a good weekend."

"Yes, it's sure to be a good one," he muttered, feeling discouraged. "I'm on duty from Saturday through to Sunday. It'll probably be mayhem. In this weather. I can't remember what cold feels like, you know."

"Have a good shift, then." She smiled, heading for the door.

An occasional beer on Fridays with the old gang from police college, the summer party, and Christmas dinner. That was the contact she had with her colleagues, socially and outside office hours. Pleasant and rather distant. She parked her motorcycle, slightly doubtful about leaving it so exposed in the middle of Vaterland, but decided to put it to the test. For safety's sake, she used both chains, coiling them through their respective wheels and attaching them to two conveniently positioned metal posts.

Then she yanked off her helmet, ruffling her flattened hair, and climbed the stairs to the questionable joint with the most eccentric location of any pub in the entire city — literally underneath an overpass.

It was almost half past four, and the others were well under way, on half liters number two or three, judging by the level of noise. She was welcomed with applause and deafening cheers. There were no other girls there. In fact, there was nobody other than the seven police officers on the whole premises. A tiny waitress of Asiatic appearance scurried toward them from the inner recesses.

"A beer for my lady friend," bellowed Billy T., the monster who had frightened the wits out of Finn Håverstad that very morning.

"No, no," she deflected him, and ordered a Munkholm.

One minute later a Clausthaler was sitting

in front of her. It was obviously all the same to the waitress, though it certainly wasn't for Hanne. But she made no protest.

"What're you up to these days, babe?" Billy T. asked, putting his arm around her.

"You should get rid of that beard," Hanne replied, tugging the gigantic red whiskers he had acquired in record time.

He pulled back his head, feigning offense.

"My beard! My beautiful beard! You should see my boys. They were scared to death the first time they saw me with it, but now they want one themselves, every single one of them!"

Billy T. had four sons. Every second Friday he drove around the city, stopping at four different houses to pick up his boys. On Sunday evening he drove the same route to hand over four dog-tired, delighted boys to the protective custody and control of their respective mothers.

"You, Billy T., you who know everything," Hanne ventured after he, insulted by the comment about his beard, had released his grip on her shoulders.

"Ho-ho, what are you after now?" He grinned.

"No, nothing. But d'you know where you could get hold of blood? Huge quantities of blood?"

Everything was suddenly quiet, with the exception of one man in the middle of a good story who had not caught what she said. When he realized the others had, and were more interested in Hanne's question than his joke, he clutched his glass and downed his beer.

"Blood? Human blood? What's going on in your neck of the woods?"

"No, animal blood. Pig blood, for example. Or whatever, only it's from an animal. One found here in Norway, of course."

"Well, Hanne. That's quite elementary. At a slaughterhouse, naturally!"

As though she hadn't thought of that herself.

"Yes, I appreciate that, of course," she said patiently. "But can anyone at all simply stroll in and collect whatever they want? Can you buy vast quantities of blood at a slaughterhouse?"

"I remember my mother used to buy blood when I was little," the leanest of the police lads interjected. "She came home with horrible blood in a container, to make black pudding and stuff like that. Blood pancakes as well." He grimaced at the revolting childhood memory.

"Yes, I know that," Hanne said, still

146

patient. "Some slaughterhouses still have blood for sale. But wouldn't it raise eyebrows if someone came in asking for ten liters?"

"Is this these Saturday night massacres you're working on?" Billy T. inquired, more interested now. "Have you been told it's animal blood?"

"Some of it," Hanne informed him, without going into greater detail about what she meant by that.

"Check with the slaughterhouses here in the city, then, whether anyone has demonstrated a noticeable interest in blood with a discount for quantity. That shouldn't be too hard. Even for you lazybones in Homicide!"

They were no longer alone in the gloomy premises. Two women in their mid-twenties had sat down at the other end of the bar. Naturally it didn't escape the notice of seven men in their prime. A couple of them seemed especially interested, and Hanne concluded they must be the two among them who didn't have girlfriends at the moment. She took a quick peep at the women herself, and her heart sank. They were lesbians. Not that they had any characteristic, stereotypical appearance. One of them had long hair, and both of them looked fairly ordinary. Hanne Wilhelmsen, however, like all lesbians, possessed built-in radar making it possible to ascertain such things in a split second. When they suddenly leaned toward each other, discreetly exchanging a kiss, she was not the only one to know.

Hanne steamed. Public displays of affection drove her crazy, and it provoked her even more, if possible, that she had fallen into the trap of becoming so incensed.

"Carpet munchers," whispered one of the police officers, the one originally most interested in the two newcomers. The others laughed boisterously, all except Billy T. Another, a fair-haired, broad-built guy Hanne had never actually liked but simply tolerated, was seizing the opportunity to embark on some coarse joke or other, when Billy T. interrupted him.

"Cut that out," he ordered. "What those ladies are doing is none of our fuckin' business. What's more . . ."

A colossal forefinger pounded on his blond companion's chest.

"What's more, those jokes of yours are always so bloody awful. Listen to this one instead."

Thirty seconds later they erupted into laughter again. A fresh round of beers arrived at the table, but for Hanne it was now simply a case of allowing an adequate amount of time between the unfortunate episode and her own departure from the scene. Half an hour would do the trick.

Standing up, she pulled on her leather jacket, smiled at them, and wished them enjoyment of their Friday night adventures as she prepared to leave.

"Wait for a bit, darling." Billy T. grinned, grabbing her by the arm. "Give me a hug!"

She was leaning toward him with some reluctance, when he stopped in his tracks, staring directly into her eyes with a seriousness she had seldom witnessed in him.

"I like you, you know, Hanne," he murmured. Then he hugged her tight.

SATURDAY, JUNE 5

Nature was in a state of total confusion. The scent of bird cherry blossom hung heavily in the air, as at Midsummer, along all the byways, and the garden roses were already blooming. Tulip petals, normally in their full glory, were sprawling indecorously, and the flowers would be dead within a couple of days. Insects were buzzing around in the midst of all the frivolity, in a state of semiconsciousness. Pollen allergy sufferers were having a dreadful time, and even the most enthusiastic aficionados of summer glanced furtively at the sky. The sun seemed hardly to take a few hours' rest each night before springing up, just as scorching and fighting fit as ever, around five o'clock every morning. There must be something wrong somewhere.

"The comet is coming," groaned Hanne Wilhelmsen, who read Tove Jansson's Moomin books annually.

She was sitting on their little balcony with her feet on the railings, reading the Saturday newspapers. It was already almost half past ten at night but definitely too warm to sit indoors watching television.

"Wimp," Cecilie responded, offering her a glass of Campari and tonic. "In the south you would be thinking this is just marvelous. Be glad instead that for once we're having beautiful weather here in the north."

"No thanks. I've a slight headache. It must be the heat."

Cecilie was correct all the same. It was actually lovely. Hanne Wilhelmsen couldn't recall ever having sat outside in shorts and T-shirt so late into the evening and feeling too warm. Not in Norway. At least not at the beginning of June.

On the grassy slope below their balcony, two families with young children were having a party. Five children, one dog, and two pairs of parents had been barbecuing, playing singing games, and enjoying good old-fashioned outdoor fun for several hours, despite the fact it must now be well past bedtime for the youngest. An hour ago, Cecilie had wondered sotto voce how long it would take for Mrs. Weistrand on the ground floor to come out and complain. The lady in question had already banged

151

her balcony door a number of times in demonstrative protest against the children's racket. Cecilie was proved right of course. At eleven o'clock a police patrol car swung into the parking lot, and two policemen in summer uniform strode purposefully across the grass pitch toward the family idyll.

"Look at them, Cecilie," Hanne said, laughing quietly. "They're marching in step. When I was a constable, I decided I'd never do that, it looks so military. But then it's impossible to lose the habit. It's exactly like belonging to a marching band."

The policemen were peas in a pod. Two short-haired men of identical height. They stood somewhat hesitantly on the edge of the little gathering before directing themselves to the man who was apparently the elder.

"I knew it." Hanne sniggered, slapping herself on the thigh. "I knew they would approach one of the men!"

Getting to their feet, the two women leaned their elbows on the balcony railing. The group was no more than twenty meters away, and the sound carried well in the summer evening.

"Let's start packing up here," one of the two officers ordered. "We've had a complaint about a disturbance. From the neighbors, that is."

"What neighbors?"

The man who had been given the honor of being addressed flailed his arms in disappointment.

"Everybody's outside just now, you know," he said, pointing to the apartment block, where people were outside on the majority of balconies.

"We're not disturbing anybody!"

"Sorry," the officer insisted, straightening his cap. "You'll have to move indoors."

"In this heat?"

Now Mrs. Weistrand made her entrance. With a wide gait and definite sway of the hips, she stepped across from her own little patch of garden.

"It's more than two hours since I called," she scolded. "It's a disgrace."

"A lot to do, ma'am," the other twin apologized, adjusting his cap. Hanne Wilhelmsen knew it was a nightmare to wear one in this heat. She made up her mind to wade in.

"Cecilie, I really do have a headache. Could you be bothered making me some tea? You're an angel."

Tea for a headache. Good medicine, the physician surmised, knowing perfectly well why she was being asked to go inside. But

153

she said nothing, simply shrugging her shoulders as she headed for the kitchen.

"Hello," Hanne Wilhelmsen shouted over to the two officers as soon as Cecilie was out of sight. "Hello, boys!"

Everybody down on the grassy slope looked up at her. The two constables paced uncertainly in the direction of the building when they realized she was talking to them. Hanne did not know them but assumed, presumptuously enough, that they knew who she was. Which was obviously correct. When they were five meters away from her, they brightened up.

"Hello there," they both said, more or less in unison.

"Just leave them be," Hanne Wilhelmsen advised, with a wink. "They're not making any noise at all. It's the old wifey on the ground floor who's being difficult. Let the youngsters enjoy themselves."

Detective Inspector Wilhelmsen's advice was good enough for the two policemen. With a deferential touch of their caps, they turned on their heels and returned to the little gathering.

"Keep it quiet, then," one of them said as he headed with his partner toward presumably more important assignments.

Mrs. Weistrand scurried angrily back to

her burrow, while the older man at the party approached Hanne.

"Thank you very much," he said, forming his right hand into a gesture of triumph, like a "Yes-to-the-European Union" symbol from 1972.

Hanne only smiled, shaking her head. Cecilie had returned. Banging a teacup down on the table, she buried herself in the newspapers without uttering a word.

When it reached half past two, with the children long off to bed and the heat of the night sufficiently abated for them both to wear sweaters, it dawned on Hanne that Cecilie had not exchanged more than a few monosyllables with her since the police officers' visit. They remained sitting in silence, neither of them having any wish to lie down side by side, and in addition it really was a most enchanting night. Hanne had tried everything. Nothing worked. Now she was sitting wondering what in the world she should do to avoid having the entire following day spoiled as well.

Then the telephone rang. Hanne's phone.

Cecilie ripped the newspaper in two.

"If that's work, and you've got to go, I'm going to kill you," she growled indignantly before throwing the torn paper away, stamping into the apartment, and slamming the

155

bedroom door ferociously behind her. Hanne took the call.

Although she had felt mentally prepared — a phone call in the middle of the night between Saturday and Sunday never heralded anything good — she could feel the skin on her neck tighten. It was another Saturday night massacre. Håkon was phoning. He was already on the scene, a subway station in one of the older suburbs on the eastern flank of the city. It looked absolutely hellish. Since the latest information about some of the mess being human blood, he assumed she would want to take a look.

Hanne thought about it for all of ten seconds.

"I'm on my way," she said tersely.

She remained standing outside the bedroom door before knocking lightly.

"It's your room too," she heard a grumpy voice from inside.

She ventured in. Cecilie had undressed and was sitting up in bed, holding a book and wearing the ugly reading glasses she knew Hanne hated.

"You're going out, I hear," she said frostily.

"Yes, and you're coming too."

"Me?"

Lowering her book, she met Hanne's gaze

156

for the first time in hours.

"Yes. It's about time you got to see what I'm up to when I wander off outdoors during the night. This bloodbath is probably no worse than your own operating rooms."

Cecilie did not believe her. She began to read again but was clearly more preoccupied with what Hanne was about to say.

"I mean it, my friend. Put on your clothes. We're going to inspect a crime scene. Hurry up."

Five minutes later, a rose-colored Harley roared toward the Oppsal area. When they arrived, it looked quite different from the other scenes. Three patrol cars were parked, blue lights flashing, probably without causing any degree of embarrassment to the neighbors, who were straining their necks to follow what was happening anyway. The subway station was of the unmanned type, surrounded by a fence and with a contraption resembling a sluice gate facing the street on the side used by exiting passengers. The bloodbath was on the opposite side, where travelers had to walk through a small building to access the boarding platform. There were thirteen police officers in the area, Håkon Sand among them, dressed in full uniform. Hanne remembered that he was on duty. He beamed when he caught

157

sight of her greeting him as she crossed the crime scene tape draped in all directions. Cecilie had accompanied her, unchallenged by the female police sergeant guarding the perimeter.

"You were quick," he commented, apparently not noticing she had someone with her. Hanne did not introduce them.

"A young couple on their way from a party discovered it," Håkon explained. "They were madly in love and were looking for a discreet place to go."

He pointed to a corner formed by a two-meter-high wall where it met the drab gray building. The ground was a mixture of extremely old asphalt and a great many dandelions that had conquered the dark-gray surface. Now it was all black with blood. Huge quantities of blood.

"Now we're making an effort to gather evidence far more thoroughly," he explained, indicating the scene around him.

Sensible. Just what she would have done. Looking around, she spotted Hilde Hummerbakken of the dog patrol. She had put on about thirty kilos since leaving police training college and was waddling around in a far-too-tight uniform. She had, however, the most beautiful dog in the world. Its tail wagging like a propeller, it roamed over the site, stopping sometimes here, sometimes there, all the while obeying the soft-spoken, forthright commands of its mistress — a fascinating sight. After several minutes, the rotund officer approached them, and Hanne crouched down to pet the dog.

"The perpetrator must have come through the building," Hummerbakken said, panting. "That's quite clear. There's nothing along the fence. Cairo has ranged through the whole building but is picking up something thirty meters up the slope there. He or she had a car. Should these buildings not be locked at night?"

"Probably," Hanne Wilhelmsen said as she stood up. "But with fewer and fewer staff, there's a limit to how meticulous they can be. There's nothing here to steal. Just an empty building."

Police Inspector Hummerbakken left them to walk another round with the dog. Hanne Wilhelmsen borrowed a flashlight. In the middle of the bloody site, someone had placed a little strip of cardboard, like a gangway, without any rhyme or reason. She stepped carefully across as far as it reached, confirming that here too there was an eight-digit number scratched on the blood-smeared wall. Then she turned to the others, hunkered down, and looked around in every direction.

"As I thought," she muttered, getting to her feet and making her way back.

None of them understood what Hanne had established. Cecilie was dumbstruck by all the impressions bombarding her and had not yet recovered from the fact that she was actually standing there, in the midst of a buzzing nest filled with Hanne's colleagues.

"In there, near the wall, you could have four square meters where you are invisible," she enlightened them. "The nearest building you see is that one over there. In this light, it's impossible for anyone out there to see in here."

They followed her index finger to a building shrouded in darkness on a low elevation, at least three hundred meters distant.

"Hello," Håkon Sand suddenly declared, as though he hadn't noticed Cecilie until now. He stretched out his hand. "I'm Håkon Sand."

"Cecilie Vibe." Cecilie smiled radiantly in return.

Hanne interrupted the extremely brief conversation.

"A friend of mine. She was visiting. Couldn't exactly leave her," she lied with a forced smile, immediately feeling terrible pangs of regret.

"And now you'll have to drive me home," Cecilie said, cold as ice, nodding briefly in Håkon's direction and starting to head for the door of the gray building.

"No, wait, Cecilie," Hanne said desperately.

In a loud voice, to be sure her partner would hear, she addressed herself to Håkon: "Actually, I was thinking of inviting you to dinner next Friday. At my place, that is. With my partner. Then you can meet . . ."

She swallowed the word "her."

". . . my partner," she concluded without thinking how odd the repetition must sound.

The police attorney looked as though he had been invited on a three-week cruise in the Caribbean. Just as incredulous and evidently just as happy.

"But of course," he replied, without even considering that he had actually arranged to see his aging mother. "Certainly! We can discuss the details later!"

Leaving the bloodbath behind, Hanne followed Cecilie away from the scene and across to the motorcycle. She said nothing. She felt numb and had no idea how she would get herself out of the arrangement she had just made.

161

"So that was Håkon Sand. He seems pleasant enough," Cecilie prattled. "I think you ought to tell him about me before he turns up."

She leaned her head back and laughed uproariously before her gloomy surroundings crossed her mind, and she stopped abruptly. Then she chuckled all the way home.

Sunday, June 6

At last the newspapers had jumped aboard. It genuinely delighted him. When the church bells had roused him around ten o'clock, after four short, but sound, hours' sleep, he had thrown on a jogging suit and headed for the gas station to see if anyone other than the police was finally beginning to take an interest in his actions.

It was almost more than he could hope for. The entire front page of *Dagbladet* was emblazoned with the headline MYSTERIOUS BLOODBATH IN OSLO, with the subheading POLICE SEARCHING FOR VICTIMS. A tiny photograph in the corner showed a police car, some crime scene tape, and five police officers. It was small in comparison with the headline, but perhaps the blood-drenched corner would not make a good photograph in itself. It would have to be in color at the very least.

Next time, perhaps, he thought before going to take his second shower in five hours. Next time.

They felt like participants in a mediocre American TV film. They were lying in a typical bachelor pad on a tasteless, gigantic white-painted bed, with a tilted headboard containing a built-in radio and alarm clock. But the mattress was good. Hauling himself up, Håkon shyly pulled on his underpants and shuffled through to the kitchen. A moment later he returned with two glasses of cola clinking with ice cubes, and a lopsided smile.

"He's a good guy, you know."

His friend had become accustomed to it by now. This was the fourth time Håkon had blushingly asked to borrow his apartment for a few hours. The first time, his friend was at a loss to understand why Håkon couldn't take his sex partner to his own place, but in the end he had grinned and handed over the keys.

"We all have peculiar predilections," he announced, assuring Håkon that he would stay away for five hours.

Since then, the friend hadn't even passed any comment, simply handing over the keys with an instruction about how long he could stay. This time, however, he had asked if there wasn't anyone else with an apartment he could borrow, as it wasn't at all convenient. But when he saw Håkon's face, he immediately changed his mind. What he did not know was he was not the only one who received this peculiar request from Håkon Sand at regular intervals.

It would not be long until they could expect the owner's return. Håkon looked discreetly at the clock, but not discreetly enough.

"Yes, I know," she said. "We have to get up."

As she made a move, she suddenly declared, "I'm sick and tired of having to meet like this."

As though it were his choice. He chose not to respond.

"In fact, I'm sick and tired of most things," she continued as she put on her clothes with exaggerated, hasty movements.

"I'm thinking of ending it."

Håkon Sand could feel his temper coming to a boil.

"Oh, yes. With this situation here? Or with smoking, perhaps?"

She smoked too much, and if it hadn't actually started to irritate him, he was at least worried on her behalf. He assumed, however, it wasn't tobacco she was thinking

165

of cutting out. It was him. She mentioned this in passing around every third time they were together. Earlier, it had terrified him and made him totally desperate. Currently, it only made him completely pissed off.

"Listen, Karen," he said. "You can't go on like this. You have to make up your mind now. Do you want me or don't you?"

The woman came to a sudden stop, then walked around the bed, fastening her trousers.

"You know," she said, smiling, "I didn't mean you. Not us. I was talking about my work. I think I should pack in my job."

That was even more mind-boggling. He plunked himself down on the edge of the bed. Pack in her job? She was the youngest partner in a renowned legal firm, earning astronomical sums of money as far as he could make out, and had very rarely expressed anything to indicate she did not enjoy it.

"Oh, well" was all he said.

"What do you think?"

"No, I th—"

"Forget it."

"I didn't mean it like that! I'd like to talk about it."

"No, forget it. Honestly. We won't discuss it just now. Another time, perhaps."

She plumped herself down beside him.

"I'm thinking of going to the cottage on Friday. Do you want to come?"

Sensational. She wanted to take him with her to the cottage. Two and a half days together. The entire time. Without having to hide. Without having to get up and go their respective ways after making love. Sensational.

"I'd really like to," he stammered, realizing in the same second that her cottage no longer existed. He had a long, nasty wound on his leg from when the building had burned to the ground six months earlier. The scar was still painful on bad days.

"It'll be a bit too airy, don't you think?" he said drily.

"Not my cottage. My neighbor's. And then we can tidy up the site and enjoy ourselves in between times."

Then he realized one more thing. He had accepted the surprise invitation to dinner at Hanne Wilhelmsen's.

"Oh, shit."

"What is it?"

"I've got an appointment. Dinner date. Hanne Wilhelmsen has invited me to her apartment."

"Hanne? I thought you never saw each other outside office hours?"

Karen Borg knew Hanne Wilhelmsen. She had encountered her a few months before, and the policewoman had made a deep impression. Moreover, Håkon could hardly tell a story about his work without the detective inspector being mentioned. But she had never considered them as anything more than colleagues.

"We never have. Until now. She invited me last night, in fact."

"Can you not call off?" she suggested, running her hands through his hair.

For a fraction of a second, a "Yes of course" reached the tip of his tongue. Then he shook his head. It was one thing to dump his mother in favor of Hanne. Family was somehow different. But he couldn't say no to Hanne simply because a more attractive option had cropped up.

"No, I can't do that, Karen. I've said I'd really like to come."

A silence fell between them. Then she smiled and pressed her mouth to his ear. He could feel shivers all the way down his neck.

"You're a good guy," she whispered. "A lovely, dependable good guy."

The young mother with flying red hair was falling apart completely. Her little boy was nowhere to be found. She was running haphazardly to and fro in the narrow streets of the old, rundown residential area, leaning over every single hedge, shouting desperately.

"Kristoffer! Kristoffer!"

She had dozed off in the warm weather. When she last saw him they had just finished eating dinner. Meatballs with sour cabbage. The three-year-old just wanted to eat mashed potatoes with sauce. It was too hot to argue with a toddler at the defiant stage. Moreover, it was Sunday, and she needed some peace and quiet.

After eating, she had picked up a book and stretched out on the sun bed just behind the charming old house they rented from her uncle. Full of drafts and rather dilapidated, it was not what you would call child-friendly, but the rent was peanuts and the surrounding area was quiet and traffic-free. She had put the boy into the sandpit her uncle had kindly set up in the garden behind the house. He had been jabbering away and having a great time. And then she must have fallen asleep.

Now she was consumed with desperation and full of tears. She tried to convince herself he couldn't possibly have gone far in the half hour or so she had been snoozing.

"Think," she said determinedly to herself, clamping her jaws together. "Think! Where does he usually go? Where is it exciting and forbidden to go?"

Terror-stricken at the first answer that struck her, she stopped in her tracks and wheeled around to face the freeway rushing by, three hundred meters below the hillside with all the tiny old houses and gardens. No. He couldn't have gone there. He just couldn't have.

An elderly woman in a pinafore and gardening gloves was standing beside a hedge as she rounded the corner of the street about a hundred and fifty meters from home.

"Have you lost Kristoffer?" she asked kindly and somewhat superfluously, since the young woman had been calling her son's name all the way.

"Yes. No. Not lost. I just can't find him."

Her submissive, strained smile encouraged the older woman to pull off her gloves resolutely.

"Come on. I'll help you. He's probably not gone far," she consoled her.

They made an odd couple as they continued the pursuit. The nervous red-haired woman running from one side to the other through the streets on long, freckled legs.

The older lady more systematic, striding up to every single house, taking time to ask the occupants if they had seen the three-year-old.

Eventually they reached the farthest edge of the hill. There was no boy to be seen, and no one else had seen him either. Only the outskirts of the forest lay ahead of the two women, one confused and anxious, the other out of her mind with worry.

"Where can he be?" Kristoffer's mother sobbed. "He wouldn't dare go into the forest by himself. Perhaps he's gone downhill? To the freeway."

The very thought convulsed her with tears.

"There, there. Take it easy. Let's not assume the worst. If anything had happened down there, we'd have heard the ambulance long ago," the older woman comforted her, without any real sense of logic.

"Mommy!"

Beaming with pleasure, a boy came toddling on little suntanned legs out along a garden path, bucket in one hand and plastic spade in the other. If it could be called a garden path. The house nearest to the forest had been unoccupied for a decade, something the property clearly showed. If it hadn't been for the entrance being covered in a thick layer of fine-grained gravel, it would have merged completely into the overgrown garden.

"Kristoffer," hiccupped the mother, dashing toward him.

Surprised by the intensity of their reunion, he allowed himself to be lifted up and cuddled until he could scarcely breathe.

"I've found a pirate, Mommy," he announced, proud and excited. "A real pirate!"

"That's wonderful, my darling boy," his mother replied. "Wonderful! But you must promise me never to go so far away again. Mommy was very scared, you see. Now we'll go home and have some juice. I think you must be quite thirsty."

She gazed at the other woman with heartfelt thanks.

"Many thanks, Mrs. Hansen. Many, many thanks. I was so worried."

"Yes, it's okay, no problem." Mrs. Hansen smiled, taking the boy's hand to accompany the little family home.

"I want to show you the pirate, Mommy," he protested, tearing himself away from both women. "You've got to see my pirate."

"Not today, sweetheart. We can go home to your pirate ship and play with that instead."

The little boy's bottom lip began to

quiver. "No, Mommy. I want to see the real pirate!"

He stood straddle-legged and defiant in the middle of the road, refusing to budge.

Mrs. Hansen intervened. "We'll go now and have a look at your pirate for a little while and then you and your mommy can come home with me. We'll have a nice time. Won't we?"

The final comment was directed at the young woman. She smiled again gratefully, clasping the boy's hand, and all three of them entered the overgrown garden. Truth to tell, both adults were somewhat curious about what the boy had found.

Even on a bright, shining Sunday afternoon, the house seemed rather frightening. The paint work had flaked off in most places a long time ago. Someone, probably teenagers who didn't have anything better to do, had smashed all the windows. That had been years before, and even those young restless souls had lost interest in the building — it was now easy prey for the ravages of time. Stinging nettles grew virtually waist-high in some parts of the garden. But around the back, where hardly anyone had been in several years, some kind of grassy lawn was fighting for its life and was managing to stand its ground reasonably well at present. Although there were grassy lawns and grassy lawns. This looked more like a meadow.

When they rounded the corner, the little boy ran across to a small toolshed at the other end of the garden. His mother was afraid the boy would enter the half-open door and called out a warning. It wasn't necessary. The boy wasn't going inside. He crouched down on his haunches beside one of the walls, smiling uncommonly proudly at the two grown-ups, and used his spade to point down into a little hole as he exclaimed loudly, "Look! There's my pirate!"

It was a human head.

Intuitively grabbing the boy, the younger woman retreated several meters from the spot.

He was bawling. "I want to see! I want to see!"

Mrs. Hansen took only a few seconds before quietly taking command of the situation. "Get him away from here. Tell my husband to call the police. I'll stay here. Hurry!"

She added the last word when the red-haired mother of the toddler, perplexed and almost paralyzed, remained rooted to the spot, staring at the hole in the ground. She pulled herself away from the grotesque sight and ran off carrying the yelling and kicking toddler, leaving the bucket and spade lying on the grass.

Kristoffer had dug up an area of around forty square centimeters. The head was not buried deeply, at most thirty centimeters. Mrs. Hansen had difficulty understanding how the boy had managed to dig so far. An animal might have made a start on the job.

It might be a woman. It looked like it. The lower part of the face was tightly wrapped in a piece of cloth that seemed to be tied around her head. The corpse's mouth was open, so the teeth on the upper jaw had forced themselves forward over the binding. Underneath the fabric she could clearly see a depression where the mouth had formed itself into a large O. The nostrils were unusually large and filled with earth. Only one eye was visible. It was half closed. There was a dark, encrusted lock of hair across the other eye, so flat and straight it resembled a head band sitting askew. Almost like a pirate.

Just a few minutes later, Mrs. Hansen heard the police sirens approaching. Standing upright, she stiffly stroked the painful varicose veins on her legs before heading toward the gate to direct the police to the grave.

MONDAY, JUNE 7

Hanne Wilhelmsen was desperate. A grisly murder was absolutely the last thing she needed now. She protested so vehemently that the superintendent almost allowed her to be spared yet again. But only almost.

"There's nothing to discuss, Hanne," he said finally in a tone of voice that brooked no opposition. "We all have too much on our plates. You are taking on this case."

She was on the brink of tears. In order to avoid doing something she would later regret, she silently gripped the papers he handed her and left his office without another word. Once she had returned to her own office, she took a few deep breaths, closing her eyes and suddenly realizing this could offer a pretext to wriggle out of the dinner engagement with Håkon Sand on Friday. So it would be good for something after all.

The body had been, as old Mrs. Hansen

presumed, that of a woman. On superficial examination at the discovery scene, she had struck Hanne as being somewhere in her early twenties, five foot three, of foreign origin, naked apart from a strip of cloth pulled tightly across her mouth, and with her throat cut. The hot weather and the fact that she had not been covered in either plastic or clothes had made it difficult to determine the exact time of death. The corpse was probably in a greater state of decomposition than it would have been under other circumstances. The extremely provisional hypothesis was that it must have been lying there for a fortnight. Forensics had instructed soil samples to be taken, together with exact measurements of the depth at which she had been buried. A somewhat more precise assessment of the time of death would be available fairly soon. The body would also be examined to determine whether a sexual attack had taken place. If the woman had been murdered immediately after sexual intercourse, it was possible semen could remain in the vagina for a lengthy period.

Hanne Wilhelmsen grabbed the Polaroid photograph of the woman's neck. The cut had the characteristic appearance of an incision wound started with a stab. Normal knife wounds were most often simply stab wounds, like small elliptical boats from which the innards had a disgusting tendency to protrude. Slicing wounds shared the same characteristics but were longer and wider. Thinner toward each end, wider at the middle. Boat shaped. However, this wound was produced by first stabbing the knife in just below one ear. The wound there was gaping and slightly jagged, as though the killer had needed to stab several times to get a good grip. After that, a penetrating arc encircled the entire neck — an even, diminishing fissure with clean edges.

They had no idea who she was. They checked all the missing person reports for the past year, despite its being an undoubtedly fresh corpse. None of the descriptions matched.

Hanne Wilhelmsen's head started to swim. After an incident a few months earlier when she had been struck down by an assailant immediately outside her own office, sustaining a serious concussion, she had experienced attacks of dizziness. Especially in this heat. The amount of work she had to do certainly didn't improve matters. She supported herself on the edge of the desk until the worst was over, then stood up and left the room. It was half past eight. A new workweek was off to the worst possible start.

Beside the staircase, extending from the ground to the seventh floor at the western corner of the foyer, Håkon Sand was standing talking to a colleague. He was wearing his best clothes and looked very uncomfortable in them. One of the large official black business cases was at his feet.

He brightened somewhat when he caught sight of Hanne and ended his conversation with his colleague, who disappeared across the gallery toward the yellow zone.

"I'm looking forward to Friday." He beamed broadly.

"Me too," she replied, trying to make it sound truthful.

They remained standing there, leaning over the railings and peering down at the enormous open room beneath them. On one side there was an unusual scarcity of people.

"Obviously no one's needing a passport these days," Håkon Sand remarked in an effort to explain that the ladies at the passport windows, usually so busy, were now sitting chatting. "In that case it's a good time for a jaunt to Alaska. Or Svalbard.

"But of course you don't need a passport to go there," he added, embarrassed.

If there were few Norwegians requiring

passports, it was all the more crowded at the other end of the room. Foreigners were sitting crammed together along the wall where the immigration police were situated. They seemed glum, but at least they weren't much bothered by the heat.

"What on earth are they up to down there?" Hanne asked. "Are they holding a count of all the immigrants, or what?"

"Not quite. They're carrying out one of these crazy campaigns of theirs again. Going out on a trawl of public places, hauling in everybody with black hair to check if they're here lawfully. Excellent use of resources. Especially now."

He sighed. He had to be in court in twenty minutes.

"The head of CID claims there are more than five thousand illegal foreigners here in the city. Five thousand! I don't believe that for a moment. Where are they, then?"

Hanne Wilhelmsen did not think the campaign was so wide of the mark. What she reacted against was the use of sorely needed resources to find them. The other day she had heard the boss of the Immigration Directorate mention on the *Dagsnytt Atten* news program that they "lost" fifteen hundred asylum seekers every year — people they had registered coming into the country but of whom they had seen nothing subsequently. That meant there were only three and a half thousand extra, of course, she thought wearily.

"Half of them seem to be down there," she said in a tardy response to his question, indicating the flock of people below.

Håkon Sand glanced at his watch. He was busy.

"We'll catch up later," he shouted as he took to his heels.

It was all a trivial matter. Two immigrants had come to blows in an argument about food at the Urtegata Reception Center for Asylum Seekers. One an Iranian, the other a Kurd. Håkon Sand didn't think it at all strange they exploded now and again. Both of them had waited for more than a year for their applications to be processed. Both were young men in their most employable years. They were offered five hours of Norwegian lessons per week, and the remainder of their time was a sea of frustration, uncertainty, and tremendous anxiety.

Their paths had crossed one Friday evening, resulting in a broken nose for the weaker of the two, the Kurd. Article 229 of the Penal Code, paragraph 1, first penalty option. Although the Iranian boy had been given a proper black eye himself, zealous police officers were ensuring that even in this trifling case, justice would be meted out to the maximum. He was represented by a lawyer from Legal Aid, who probably had barely spoken to him, far less read the documents. But it followed the usual routine. For Håkon Sand as well.

Courtroom 8 was tiny and dilapidated. There was no air-conditioning, and the hubbub from the street made it impossible to have the windows open. After it had been decided several years earlier, at long last, to build a new courthouse, it was evidently out of the question to spend as much as a cent on the old building. Even though they were taking their time with the new one.

The black cap, used by hundreds of prosecutors before him, smelled foul. He sighed in dismay, snatching a glance at the attorney beside the other counter. As their eyes met, they made a silent agreement to have the case over and done with quickly.

The twenty-two-year-old from Iran gave his statement first. An interpreter with a completely expressionless face translated what he was saying. Obviously in an edited summary — first the accused spoke for three minutes, and then the interpreter translated for thirty seconds. Such things usually irritated Håkon Sand, but today he couldn't be bothered. Soon it was the Kurd's turn. His nose was still crooked, having hardly been on the receiving end of the best treatment the Norwegian health service could provide.

In conclusion, a member of staff from the reception center entered and gave his statement. A Norwegian. He had seen the fight. The accused had set upon the victim. They had struck each other several times before it all ended with the Kurd falling to the ground like a sack of potatoes after an impressive uppercut from the other man.

"Did you intervene?" the defense counsel asked when it was his turn to question the witness. "Did you make any attempt to come between them?"

The Norwegian stared down at the booth where he was standing, slightly embarrassed. He had not actually done so. They were a bit scary, these fights between foreigners. It happened quite often that knives came into the picture. He looked at the two judges for support but received only blank stares.

"Did you see any knife?"

"No."

"Did you have any other grounds for believing knives would be involved?"

"Yes, you see, as I said, it usually always —"

"But did you see any in this situation?" the defense counsel broke in, irritated. "Was there something in particular about this fight that made you decide not to intervene?"

"No, not really —"

"Thank you, no further questions."

The proceedings were concluded in twenty minutes. Håkon Sand packed up his papers in the knowledge that a sentence would be dished out this time too. As he was placing the slim bundle of documents into his business case, a pink form fell on the floor. It was an internal instruction from the investigator. Picking it up, he glanced at the contents before replacing the form in the file.

At the top was his name. The instruction was handwritten. The heading read: "Concerning refugee number 90045621, Shaei Thyed, assault charge."

Suddenly he understood. The numbers scratched into the blood at all the Saturday night massacres. They were of course immigration control numbers. All foreigners had them. FK numbers.

A beautiful version of the Goddess of Justice

stood on his desk. Splendid and pricey, the bronze sculpture seemed out of place inside a cramped eight-square-meter, extremely public office. He sat laying small paper pellets on each of the two scales the lady held on her outstretched arm. They rocked from side to side from the minuscule weight.

Eventually Hanne Wilhelmsen arrived, noting the new curtains with satisfaction.

"I thought you were in court," she said. "It looked that way this morning."

"It took an hour and a half," he answered, inviting her to take a seat. "I've discovered the solution!"

Håkon Sand's red cheeks were not caused by the heat.

"Those numbers written in blood at all the Saturday night massacres, do you know what they are?"

Hanne Wilhelmsen gazed at Håkon Sand for twenty seconds. Excited and ready to burst, he was terribly disappointed when she replied, "FK numbers!"

She stood up abruptly, clenching her fist and pummeling the wall several times. "But of course! Where have we been? We're drowning in these numbers, of course!"

Håkon Sand could not comprehend how it had dawned on her before he had even uttered a word. The astonishment in his eyes was so obvious she realized she had to give him some credit.

"We haven't been able to see the forest for the trees. Honestly, I haven't paid much attention to these numbers. Until now. Brilliant, Håkon! I wouldn't have thought of it by myself. Not today, at least."

Håkon did not ask any more questions and swallowed his own injured pride. They both put their minds to the consequences of their discovery. Neither of them said anything.

Four bloodbaths. Four different numbers. Immigration control numbers. One body found. Presumably a foreigner. Someone with an immigration control number.

"There may be three more of them," Håkon Sand said finally. "Three more bodies. In the worst-case scenario."

In the worst-case scenario. Hanne Wilhelmsen was totally in agreement. But there was another aspect of this case that frightened her almost more than the fact that there might be three more bodies out there, someplace or other, dead and buried.

"Who has access to information about asylum seekers, Håkon?" she asked softly, although she knew the answer well.

"The personnel in the Immigration Directorate," he replied promptly. "And in the

Justice Department, of course. Quite a number.

"Plus those who work in the reception centers, I expect," he added, at the thought of the shamefaced Norwegian who had stood quietly watching two asylum seekers tearing strips off each other without intervening.

"Yes," she said.

But she was thinking about something completely different.

All other cases were put on ice in the meantime. With an efficiency that amazed most of those involved, the section's resources were reorganized in less than an hour. The operations room at the far end of the blue zone suddenly became a center of buzzing activity. There was nonetheless too little time to cancel the meeting the superintendent insisted upon, and they therefore assembled in the conference room, which was extremely convenient, since the room with no windows was also pressed into service as the dining room, and it was lunchtime.

The head of CID, round as a ball and with an infinitely naïve facial expression under his thin gray curls, was also present. He was sitting munching an enormous sandwich.

187

Mayonnaise trickled out between the two slices of bread, and the white liquid dropped like a fat, revolting larva on his much-too-tight uniform trousers. Embarrassed, he wiped it up with his index finger, attempting to minimize the damage by rubbing the dark stain. It grew even larger.

"This is rather serious," the superintendent began.

He was an extremely handsome man, athletic and broad shouldered, with a dark, short circlet of hair around a completely bald pate. His eyes were strikingly deep set but on closer inspection were large, intense, and very dark brown. He wore a pair of pale-colored summer trousers and a tight-fitting polo shirt with collar and studs at the front.

"Arnt?"

The man invited to speak moved his chair back from the table but did not stand up.

"I've checked the FK numbers in the blood. They weren't absolutely clear in all places, but if we arrive at the following interpretation . . ."

Withdrawing a sheet of card, he held it up.

". . . and this is the most likely interpretation, then they are all numbers belonging to women."

The room fell silent.

"They are all between twenty-three and twenty-nine years of age. None of them arrived in Norway accompanied. None had relatives here previously. And furthermore . . ."

They knew what he was about to say. The superintendent felt the sweat running down his temples. The head of CID was snorting like a bulldog in the heat. Hanne Wilhelmsen wanted most of all to leave.

"They have all disappeared."

After a lengthy pause that none of them found strange, the superintendent spoke up again.

"Might the body be one of these four?"

"It's too early to say. But naturally that's what we're working on."

"Erik, have you made any progress in the search for the blood?"

The constable stood up, unlike his more experienced colleague Arnt.

"I've phoned all the slaughterhouses," he said, swallowing nervously. "Twenty-four places. Blood can be bought by anyone at all. Mostly cow's blood. The majority of sales require provisional advance notice. The market has all but disappeared. Nobody makes their own black pudding anymore, it seems. No one has reported anything unusual. That is to say, no high-volume sales."

"Very well," the superintendent responded. "Do more work on the case, all the same."

Relieved, Erik Henriksen plopped himself back down on the chair.

"The boss of the Immigration Directorate," Hanne Wilhelmsen mumbled.

"What did you say?"

"The boss of the Immigration Directorate," she repeated, louder this time. "I heard an interview with him on the radio not so long ago. He said the authorities 'lose' fifteen hundred asylum seekers every year."

"Lose?"

"Yes, they go away, it seems. Most of them are expulsion cases, apparently, something they know about already. The Directorate of Immigration thinks they run away without telling anyone. To Sweden, perhaps, or farther south in Europe. Some of them quite simply return home. At least that's what the boss of the Immigration Directorate thought."

"Does nobody look for them?" Erik asked, regretting his question immediately. That the immigration authorities should spend time looking for missing foreigners when they had their hands full throwing the remaining ones out of the country was such an absurd thought that the most experienced officers in the room would have laughed out loud, had it not been for present circumstances. And the heat. And the fact that they knew they had almost exactly five days left to get to the bottom of the mystery. If they didn't want to have to investigate, next Saturday night, yet another pool of blood somewhere with a new FK number drawn in all the crimson mess.

Five days was what they had. It would be best to get to work.

Kristine Håverstad felt she was approaching an abyss. Nine days had passed. Nine days and eight nights. She had not spoken to anyone. There had of course been the odd exchange of words with her father, but it still seemed that they were circling around each other. Deep inside, each of them knew full well the other wanted to talk, but how they might begin, how they would continue, for that matter, they had no idea. They could not manage to break in or out of what bound them closely together and at the same time made it so impossible for them to communicate. There was one victory she could record. The Valium had gone down the toilet. Alcohol had taken its place. Her father had watched her with a look of concern, but without any protest, as his stock of red wine dwindled and she asked him to please buy some more. The next day, two cases of wine had been sitting in the kitchen larder.

Her friends had telephoned, expressing anxiety. She hadn't been to the lecture theater for a week, her first absence in four years. She managed to pull herself together then, speaking in a lighthearted tone, complaining about a bad case of influenza and reassuring them, no, she didn't need them to visit, they would only become infected themselves. There was nothing more to say about it. She could not bear the thought of the attention that would be her fate. The memory was all too fresh of the veterinary student who had returned to the lecture theater two years earlier after a few days' absence. The girl had told her closest friends she had been raped by a medical student after a fairly lively party. A short time later, it was common knowledge. The case was dropped by the police, and the veterinary student had drifted about like a dried flower ever since. At that time, Kristine had felt very sorry for the girl. She had grumbled about it with her friends and given a wide berth to the accused bigmouth from Bærum. They had never, however, taken the initiative with the victim. On the contrary, there seemed to be something tacky about her, something unreasonable and irrational. They believed her, of course, at least the girls did, but she moved around bewildered, somehow, with something about her, something that made it best to keep away from her.

Kristine Håverstad did not want to be like her.

Worst of all was seeing her father. The strong, strapping man who had always been there, always the first person she had run to when the world got too tough. The feeling of guilt about all the times she hadn't turned to him, when something was fantastic and there was something to be celebrated, came surging out from nooks and crannies deep inside. She had never considered what kind of burden it must have been for him to be alone with her. The knowledge that she was responsible, when all was said and done, for preventing him from hooking up with a new woman had always been there. But she felt this was justified: she had been a small child and had to be shown consideration. She did not want a new mother. It had not dawned on her until she was an adult herself that he might have needed a new wife. She was deeply

193

ashamed.

The worst thing was not the feeling of being destroyed. The worst thing was the feeling that her father was.

She had gone to see the social worker. The woman had looked like a social worker and acted like a social worker but had obviously thought of herself as a psychiatrist. It was useless. If it hadn't been for Kristine Håverstad knowing how important it was not to give up immediately, she would have quit by now. But she would give it a chance.

First of all she was going to take a trip to their summer cottage. She did not take much with her. She would be gone for only a few days. Max. She could buy food at the local grocery store.

Her father had appeared almost happy when she told him yesterday evening. He had given her a generous sum of money, encouraging her to stay there for a while. He had a great deal to do at work anyway, he said, helping himself to another portion of supper. He had lost weight in the past week. She saw that his clothes were hanging slightly more loosely. Moreover, his face looked different: not exactly thinner, but the features were sharper now, the lines deeper. She too had lost three kilos. Those were three kilos she didn't have to lose.

Almost in an effort to please her father, she decided to make the journey, although she didn't really want to. Her boss had been quite annoyed when she called to say that her illness was lingering, and she would not be able to come back to work for another few days. Her job as a relief worker with the Blue Cross was neither well paid nor particularly exciting, and she couldn't quite explain why she had stayed for more than a year. She liked the alcoholics, that might be why. They were the most grateful people in the world.

Central Station was crowded with people. She had to stand in a queue for nearly twenty minutes before the number on the LCD screen matched the number on her ticket. She received what she asked for, paid, and sauntered out into the actual passenger hall. There were still ten minutes to wait before her train would leave.

Crossing the terminal, she entered the Narvesen kiosk. The tabloid newspapers had virtually identical front pages — a woman's body found in a secluded garden. She read that the police were devoting all the resources they had. She could imagine that. At least they weren't working on her case. That same morning she had phoned Linda Løvstad, her victim support counsel,

195

to hear if there was any news. The attorney had been apologetic — there was nothing to report. But she promised to let her know.

Picking up a copy of *Arbeiderbladet,* Kristine Håverstad placed the correct amount of money on the counter and headed for the platform. She skimmed the newspaper as she walked and almost tripped over a discarded hot dog wrapper. To avoid that happening again, she folded her paper and tucked it into her own bag.

That was when she saw him. Shocked and completely paralyzed, she remained standing there for a few seconds without moving a muscle. It was him. The rapist. Large as life, strolling around Oslo Central Station on a hot Monday in June. He didn't look at her, just walked, talking to the man accompanying him. He was evidently saying something amusing, as the other man leaned his head back and laughed out loud.

A violent trembling began around her knees, creeping up over her thighs, and making it difficult for Kristine Håverstad to reach a bench, where she collapsed with her back to the rapist. But it wasn't simply being confronted with his actual existence that shocked her.

What was more appalling was that she now knew where to get hold of him.

■ ■ ■ ■

At almost exactly the same time, Kristine's father was in his daughter's apartment, looking out the window. The apartment block directly opposite was not renovated like hers. Large flakes of plaster had fallen off the façade, and there were two broken windows. Nevertheless, all the apartments appeared to be inhabited, and several of them looked attractive, at least from this distance. There was no movement to be detected anywhere. Most were probably at work. At one of the windows, on the second floor diagonally opposite, to the left of where he was sitting, he could make out a shadow that looked like a man. Judging by the distance between the window ledge and his face, it appeared he was sitting in a deep chair. The man must have a perfect view down to Kristine's apartment.

Finn Håverstad stood up quickly and rushed out of the apartment. He closed the door with the main lock and the two extra security locks he had installed so ineffectually. When he emerged into the street, he hastily worked out which doorbell belonged to the apartment he had just been staring into. The doorbell did not have a nameplate, but he took a chance. The second floor on the left. The third doorbell from the bottom on the left of the two rows. There was no reply, but after a few seconds he could hear a buzz indicating that someone had pressed the door-release button. The characteristic electronic noise was clearly audible, and he tentatively attempted to push the entrance door open. It yielded easily.

The stairway was at least as dilapidated as the façade of the block suggested, but it smelled freshly of green soap. The heavily built man ascended determinedly to the second floor. The front door was blue, with a rectangle of frosted glass from doorknob level. Above the doorbell hung a little card, attached using a thumbtack with a red plastic head. E. That was what it said. E. Nothing more. He rang the bell.

There was a terrible racket inside. Then it went quiet. Håverstad tried again, followed by another explosion of sound. Suddenly the door opened. A man stood inside. It was difficult to estimate his age, as he had that peculiar, practically sexless appearance of a true eccentric. Nondescript face, neither ugly nor handsome. Hardly any beard growth. Pale, with smooth, blemish-free skin. Despite the weather, he was wearing a traditional sweater. It didn't seem to bother him in the least.

"E," he said, stretching out a cold hand. "My name is E. What do you want?"

Håverstad was so surprised by this apparition he could barely explain his errand. There wasn't much to explain in any case.

"Eh . . ." he began. "I'd just like to talk to you about something."

"About what?"

He was definitely not unfriendly, only reserved.

"I'm wondering whether you keep an eye on what's going on here in the neighborhood," Håverstad said, suitably vague.

It was clearly a shrewd move. A contented expression appeared at the corners of the man's mouth.

"Come in," he said, with something resembling a slight smile.

He stepped aside, and Håverstad crossed the threshold. The apartment was spotless. It appeared virtually uninhabited and contained very little to indicate it was indeed a home. There was a massive TV screen in one corner, with a single chair in front. There was no settee in the living room and no table. At the window, which had no curtains either, was the chair where Håverstad assumed the man had been sitting when he caught a glimpse of him from his

199

daughter's apartment. It was a well-worn green winged armchair, surrounded by several cardboard boxes of the kind he recognized from his own files. Brown archive boxes made of stiff cardboard, lined up around the chair, like erect square soldiers defending their green citadel. On top of the chair, on the seat, lay a clipboard with a pen attached.

"This is where I live," E said. "It was better where I was living before. But then my mother died, and I had to move."

At the memory, a sad expression crossed his featureless face.

"What have you got in those boxes there?" Håverstad inquired. "Are you collecting something?"

E stared at him suspiciously.

"Yes, that's what I do, in fact," he said, without making any move to elaborate on the contents of the twenty to twenty-five cardboard boxes.

Håverstad had to approach the problem from a different angle.

"You probably don't miss much, do you?" he said, showing interest, as he headed toward the window.

Although the glass showed signs of age, it was just as clean as the rest of the living quarters. There was a faint lemon scent.

"You've got a comfortable seat here," he went on without looking at the man, who had snatched up the clipboard and was now standing hugging it close, as though it was worth its weight in gold. Which perhaps it was.

"Is there anything special you're interested in?"

The sweater-clad gentleman was obviously confused. Håverstad figured not many people bothered talking to him. He evidently wanted to talk. He would take whatever time it required.

"Well, yes and no," E said in reply. "There's such a lot now, out there."

A newspaper cutting was jutting out from one of the cardboard boxes. Half the face of a female politician was smiling at him.

"Are you interested in politics?" He smiled, bending down to see what it was about.

E anticipated his move.

"Don't touch," he snarled, snapping the box closed right in front of his nose. "Don't touch my things!"

"No, of course not, of course not!"

Finn Håverstad lifted his hands, palms upward, in a gesture of surrender, wondering at the same time whether he shouldn't just leave.

"You can look at this," E said suddenly, as though he had read his thoughts and realized he was actually hungry for company regardless.

He lifted up box number two from the front and held it out to his guest.

"Film reviews," he explained.

That was what they were. Film reviews from newspapers, perfectly cut out and pasted onto A4 sheets. Underneath each review was the name of the newspaper and the date of the article, neatly inscribed with a fine, black felt-tip pen.

"Do you go to the cinema often?"

Håverstad was not especially interested in E's habits, but this was at least an opening.

"The cinema? Me? Never. But they come on the television after a while, you see. It's good to know something about them then."

Of course. A reasonable explanation. This was absurd. He ought to leave.

"You can see this too."

Now the man had become considerably more kindly disposed. He risked putting down the clipboard, even though he kept his face averted. The dentist was handed a second box. This one was heavier than the last. He looked around for somewhere to sit, but the floor was the only possibility. The clipboard was lying on the green chair, and the straight-backed chair beside the television did not invite a body such as his to sit.

He hunkered down and opened the box file. E knelt beside him, like an excited little child.

They were car registration numbers. In neat rows down the sheets of paper, divided into three columns. Each number was written down carefully below the previous one. It looked almost as though it had been typed out.

"Car numbers," E elaborated unnecessarily. "I've been collecting them for fourteen years. The first sixteen pages are from here. The rest are from where I lived . . . before."

Again he adopted that sorry, self-pitying expression, but it disappeared more quickly this time.

"Look at this." He pointed. "None of the numbers are the same. It's cheating, really. Just new numbers. Only numbers I can see from the window. Here . . ."

He pointed again.

"Here you see the date. Some days I collect around fifty numbers. Some days it's just the same ones I've got from before. At the weekends and so on. There's not much then, you see."

The sweat was pouring from Håverstad.

His heart was thumping like a fishing boat with engine trouble, and he sat right down on the actual floor to avoid the exertion of squatting.

"Have you by any chance" — he snorted — "have you by any chance some numbers from last weekend? From Saturday, May twenty-ninth?"

E pulled out a sheet and handed it to him. In the top left-hand corner was written *Saturday, May 29*. Thereafter followed seven car registrations. Only seven!

"Yes, well, it's only cars that park here, you see," E explained eagerly. "There's no point in writing down the ones that just drive past."

The dentist's hands were shaking. He felt no pleasure at all at the discovery. Only a faint, slightly numb kind of satisfaction. Almost the same as when he had carried out a successful root canal treatment without causing the patient too much discomfort.

"Could I copy down these numbers, do you think?"

E hesitated for a second, then shrugged his shoulders and stood up.

"Okay."

Half an hour later, Finn Håverstad was sitting at home faced by a list of seven car registration numbers and a telephone. Luckily, Kristine had gone to the summer cottage. He had plenty of time. Now all he had to do was find out which of these numbers corresponded to red cars. And who owned them. He called the operator and got the phone number of the vehicle registration center in Brønnøysund and five police stations in eastern Norway, and set to work.

The violent shock had subsided, and a heavy, almost liberating sense of peace had settled in its place. When, after spending a few minutes pulling herself together, Kristine had left Central Station secure in the knowledge her rapist had disappeared down one of the platforms with his companion, she remained standing near the taxi line in front of the station, looking around at the city. For the first time in more than a week, she noticed the weather in surprise. She was too warmly dressed. Pulling her sweater over her head, she stuffed it into her shoulder bag. For a moment she regretted she hadn't brought her rucksack, as it was heavy to carry this one across only one shoulder.

For once there was no queue for taxis. Everybody emerging from the station without too much luggage was doing the same as she was. Taken aback by the lovely heat after the air-conditioned passenger hall, they stretched out in the beautiful weather and decided to put their legs to use. A dark-skinned driver was standing leaning against the hood of his car, reading a foreign newspaper. She approached him, giving him her father's address and asking how much it would cost to drive there. About a hundred kroner, the man thought. She gave him a hundred-kroner note and her bag, making sure he understood the address precisely, and asked him just to leave the bag underneath the stairs.

"It's a big white house with green edges," she called through the open cab window, as he put the vehicle into gear.

A bare, hairy lower arm gave a friendly wave of reassurance from the window as the Mercedes set off.

Then she strolled toward the Homansbyen neighborhood.

She hated the man intensely. Since he had destroyed her that Saturday night an eternity of a week earlier, she had felt nothing other than powerlessness and sorrow. For hours she had wandered through the streets, overcome by a tumult of feelings she could not manage to sort out. Two days previously, she had stood in front of the railroad track above Majorstua station, right on the bend after the tunnel, invisible to everybody, even the driver of the train. She had stood there stiffly, listening to the approach of the train. Only a meter from the track. When the lead carriage suddenly came into sight around the bend, she hadn't even heard the piercing whistle. She just stood there, mesmerized, not moving a muscle, without even contemplating throwing herself onto the railroad track. The train rushed past, and the flow of air was so powerful she had needed to take a step back to keep her balance. There was only a centimeter or two between her face and the set of coaches thundering by.

She was not the one who didn't deserve to live. He was.

Now she had reached her own apartment. Hesitating for a moment at the entrance door, she let herself in.

The apartment looked just as before. It surprised her that it appeared so inviting, so comfortable. She ambled around, touching her possessions, stroking them and noticing that a light layer of dust had settled everywhere. In the dazzling light of the day outside, she saw the particles of dust dancing, as though in delight at seeing her again now that she had returned. She gingerly opened the refrigerator. It smelled slightly rank, and she emptied out the perishable foodstuffs, already starting to turn moldy. A cheese, two tomatoes, and a cucumber that squished when she grasped it. She placed the garbage bag beside the front door so she would not forget it when she left.

The bedroom door was ajar. She nervously approached the passageway, where the door, which opened out toward her, shielded her view. After a second's pause for thought, she strode resolutely into the room.

She wondered who had replaced the quilts on the bed. They were lying neatly folded with the pillows at the bottom of the mattress, beside the footboard. The bedcovers she had ripped off were gone. Of course, they would had been taken for analysis.

Almost against her will, her gaze was drawn to the two pine knobs adorning the top of each corner at the foot of the bed. Even from the door she could see the dark jagged indentations left by the steel wires that had been fastened there. They were not there now. There was nothing at all in the attractive little apartment to say what had happened there on Saturday, May 29. Except for herself.

Hesitantly, she sat on the bed. Then she leaped up, throwing the quilts on the floor and staring at the center of the mattress.

But there was nothing there either other than what she recognized from before: a few familiar stains. She sat down again.

She hated that man with all her heart. A good liberating and all-consuming hatred ran like a rod of steel along her entire spine. She had not felt it until today. Seeing the man strolling about large as life, as though nothing had happened, as though her life were something trivial he had ruined by chance one Saturday night — it was a blessing. Now she had someone to hate.

He was no longer simply an abstract monster difficult to attach a face to. Until now he hadn't been a person, just a dimension, a phenomenon. Something that had swept into her life and left it desolate, like a hurricane on the west coast or a cancerous tumor, something you could never guard against, something that visited itself on people only now and again, lamentable but completely unavoidable and out of all control.

It was no longer like that. He was a man. A person who had chosen to come. Who had chosen her life. He could have left her alone. He could have chosen not to do it, he could have decided on someone else. But she was the one he had taken. With eyes open, deliberately, on purpose.

The telephone was sitting there as usual, on a pine bedside table, beside an alarm clock and a crime novel. On a shelf just above floor height there was a phone book. She found the number rapidly and keyed in the eight digits. When she was finally connected to the place she sought, she spoke to a friendly woman.

"Hello, my name is . . . I'm Sunniva Kristoffersen," she began. "I was at East Station, no, Central Station, I mean, today. A little problem cropped up, and I was helped really well by one of your staff. He was there at half past ten. Tall, good-looking guy, very broad shoulders, blond hair, thinning slightly. I'd really like to say thank you, but I forgot to ask his name. Have you any idea who it could be?"

The woman was able to do that quite spontaneously. She gave her a name and asked if she should take a message.

"No thanks," Kristine Håverstad said quickly. "I was thinking of sending some flowers."

A few years earlier, Finn Håverstad had been at a party where he had met a reporter from *Dagsrevyen,* a well-known figure, honored with the Narvesen Prize for his pursuit of a shipowner guilty of scams using guarantee funds from the state. The man had been pleasant, and the dentist found chatting with him interesting. Before that, he had a rather hazy impression that investigative journalism consisted of secret meetings with suspect sources at odd times of the day and night. The hefty reporter had grinned when he had asked inquisitively if that were the case.

"The telephone! Ninety percent of my work comprises phone calls!"

Now he was beginning to understand that. It was amazing how much could be ascertained with the help of Bell's ingenious invention. On the notepad in front of him he now had the names of six owners of cars parked in the short little street in Homansbyen on the night between May 29 and 30.

Four of them were women. That did not need to mean anything. A husband, son or, for that matter, car thief could have been using the vehicle. But in the meantime he laid these aside. There was only one car left. He dialed the number for Romerike police station and introduced himself.

"What do you think — I was at the receiving end of some major injustice," he said indignantly to an unsympathetic policeman at the other end. "I'd parked my car beside the railroad station, and when I got back

211

the paint work was dented and scratched. Luckily a young lady had made a note of the registration number. The scoundrel hadn't left any kind of message, of course. Could you help me?"

Finally understanding the problem, the policeman jotted down the number, saying, "One moment, please," and two minutes later was able to offer him the make of car as well as the name and address of the owner. Finn Håverstad thanked him effusively.

Now he had them all. First he had tried Brønnøysund, but it was totally impossible to get through there. Apparently the easiest method was the story about being bumped. He had phoned seven police stations, thus avoiding any suspicion. It would be extremely unlikely that seven different cars had bumped him.

The only hurdle was that the vehicle color evidently was not listed in the police register. Moreover, it was probably necessary to double-check the addresses, as they could have changed since the cars were registered. To be on the safe side, he therefore phoned the National Population Register. That took an awfully long time.

But now everything was taken care of. At the Population Register he had obtained, on top of everything else, the dates of birth, something he hadn't even thought about in advance.

So four of them were women. He put them aside for the moment. One of the men was born in 1926. Far too old. Of course he might have a son the right age, but he put him to one side as well. He was then left with two. Both lived in the Oslo area, one in Bærum and one at Lambertseter.

Not even then did he actually feel any joy. On the contrary. The gnawing and the terrible pain were there beneath his heart as they had been the entire time. His skin was numb; it was as if all the feelings in his whole body had gathered in the area of his stomach. He was dreadfully exhausted. He was existing on minimal sleep. The difference was that he now had something to work on. He would find somebody to hate.

Finn Håverstad packed up his notes, stuffed them into his back pocket, and left to take a closer look at these two men.

Cecilie had accepted yet another evening at work for her partner without complaint. She was in excellent spirits. Hanne Wilhelmsen was not, however. It was almost seven o'clock, and she was sitting in the operations room with Håkon Sand and Chief

Inspector Kaldbakken. The others had gone home. Although they were working on a case of the highest urgency, there was no need to keep people there all night.

Hanne Wilhelmsen, as was her wont, had sketched out the entire case. A flip chart was spread out in the middle of the floor. The detective inspector had drawn a time line, beginning on May 8 and ending today.

Four Saturday night massacres in five weeks. None on May 29.

"It's entirely possible, of course, we simply haven't found it," Håkon Sand declared. "It might have happened all the same."

Kaldbakken looked as though he concurred, perhaps just in order to go home. He was weary, and in addition had caught a summer cold that was not exactly making his airways any easier to cope with.

"There's also another possibility," Hanne said, rubbing her face vigorously. Approaching the narrow window, she stood watching the summer evening drift over the capital city. No one said anything for quite some time.

"Now I'm fairly certain," she announced suddenly, wheeling round. "Something did happen on May twenty-ninth. But it wasn't a Saturday night massacre."

As she spoke, she became more animated,

214

as though she were persuading herself rather than aiming to enlighten the others.

"Kristine Håverstad," she blurted out. "Kristine Håverstad was raped on May twenty-ninth."

No one attempted to dispute the fact, but neither did they understand what it had to do with this case.

"We must go," she said loudly, practically shouting. "Meet me at Kristine's address!"

It obviously could not be him, the first one, the man at Lambertseter. The car was not red. On the other hand, the old man on the first floor might have made a mistake. Although he had noticed a red car, E's notes made it clear there had been several unknown cars parked at various times that night in the same area.

No, the most decisive aspect was the man's appearance. At half past five he had arrived, driving. Finn Håverstad had seen the car immediately, coming around a bend on a narrow road without asphalt in the quiet residential district. The car was newly washed, and the number plate could be read easily. Obviously busy, the man did not go to the bother of putting his car in the garage. When he emerged from the Volvo, Finn Håverstad was able to see him very

215

clearly from where he stood, fifteen meters away with an unrestricted line of sight to the recently built house.

The man was the right height, around six foot one. But he was virtually bald, with only a dark circlet of hair around a large bald crown showing he had probably not been blond since boyhood. Furthermore, he was overweight.

One left. The man in Bærum. Finn Håverstad feared it would take time, and at worst, he would not be able to take a squint at the man that day. It was already past seven o'clock in the evening, and the likelihood was the man had long since come home from work. Håverstad had placed his own car in line with the others parked along the road, which had an average amount of traffic. The address was in a terrace, with a driveway from the street into a garage at every house on the row. When he arrived, he couldn't decide where he should position himself. On foot he would probably draw attention to himself after a while, as the area was overlooked and most people were obviously heading somewhere. There was nowhere in the neighborhood where it would seem natural to spend time, no bench where he could sit with his newspaper, no playground where he could stand casually watching the children. Not that such a pastime would be such a good idea either, these days, he thought.

The problem resolved itself when a boy appeared and sat behind the wheel of a Golf parked with an excellent view of the driveway Finn Håverstad was interested in. As soon as the Golf departed, he sneaked his car into the empty space, and turning on the radio at low volume, he settled down to wait.

He had already started to hatch an alternative plan. He could ring the doorbell and ask about something. Or offer something for sale. Then he looked down at his attire and realized that by no means did he look like a salesman. Besides, he had nothing to sell.

At twenty to eight, the car arrived. A bright red Opel Astra. It had tinted glass, so Håverstad could not see the driver. The garage door had to be automatic, because as the Opel swung into the driveway, the door started to rise slowly. Slightly too slowly for the driver, who impatiently revved the motor in expectation of the aperture expanding sufficiently to enter.

Directly after the car disappeared into the garage, the man emerged, turning immediately to the opening. Håverstad saw he was holding a little gizmo in front of him, probably the remote control. The garage door slid down, and the man scurried across a little paved path toward the actual entrance of the terraced house.

It was him. It was the rapist. There wasn't a shred of doubt. For one thing, he matched Kristine's description, down to the minutest detail. Second, and far more important, Finn Håverstad could feel it in his bones. He knew the moment the man left the garage and turned around. He couldn't have had more than a glimpse of his face, but it was enough.

The father of Kristine Håverstad, brutally raped in her own residence on May 29, knew who his daughter's assailant was. He knew his name, address, and date of birth. He knew what kind of car he drove and what kind of curtains he had. He even knew he had recently cut his grass.

"Didn't you go?" he asked, incredulous, when she arrived home just as the sun was taking its leave. "I thought you were going to the cottage?"

When she turned to reply, he was pained harder than ever. She looked like a tiny bird, despite her height. Shoulders slumped and eyes disappeared somewhere inside her skull. Her mouth had an expression that reminded him more and more of his dead wife.

It was unbearable.

"Sit down for a while, then," he suggested, without waiting for her to explain the change of plan. "Sit down here for a while."

He patted the sofa beside him, but she chose the chair directly opposite. He tried desperately to make eye contact, but it was impossible.

"Where have you been?" he asked, to no avail. He went to fetch her something to drink. Surprisingly enough, she turned down the glass of red wine he offered her.

"Have we any beer?"

Have *we* any beer. She was referring to them as belonging together. That was at least something. A second later he returned, having exchanged the stemmed glass for a foaming tankard. His daughter drank half the contents in one gulp.

She had patrolled the streets for hours, but she did not mention that. She had been in her own apartment but said nothing about that either. Moreover, she had found out who had done it. But she would not tell him that.

"Out," she said softly instead. "I've been out."

Throwing out her arms expressively, she stood with her arms extended and remained frozen in a despairing pose.

"What will I do, Dad? What on earth will I do?"

Suddenly she had a powerful urge to tell him what she had seen earlier in the day. She wanted to pour it all out over him, let her father take control, responsibility, put her life in his hands. She was preparing to speak when she noticed him bend forward suddenly, head between his knees.

Kristine Håverstad had seen her father cry twice before in her life. The first time was a distant, blurred memory from her mother's funeral. The other time was only three years before, when her grandfather died unexpectedly, out of the blue, only seventy years old, after a minor prostate operation.

When she realized he was sobbing, she knew she could not tell him any of it. Instead she sat facing him and lifted his large head on to her lap.

It didn't last very long. He sat up abruptly, wiping away his tears, and cupped his hands carefully around her narrow face.

"I'm going to kill him," he said slowly.

Many times had he threatened to kill her, and other people too, when he was really annoyed. It struck her how pointless it was to say such a thing when you didn't mean it. For a dark, breathless moment she saw it plainly. This time was deadly serious. She felt terror stricken.

Agitated, Hanne Wilhelmsen had waited more than ten minutes for them, glancing at her watch every other minute while leaning against her parked motorcycle. When the others finally arrived at the newly renovated gray apartment building, the sky had a dark-blue, almost indigo hue, indicating that the following day would be equally radiant.

"Look at this," she said when Kaldbakken and Håkon Sand, having managed at last to install the unmarked police car in a tiny space, approached the spot where she stood waiting fretfully beside the entrance. "Look at that name there."

She pointed at the doorbell with its name tag untidily attached, just a scrap of paper taped on the glass.

"Asylum seeker. All on her lonesome."

She rang the doorbell, but there was no response. She rang again. Still no answer. Kaldbakken cleared his throat impatiently, unable to fathom why he was required to travel here so late in the evening. If Hanne

221

Wilhelmsen had something important to impart concerning the case, she could have come out with it at the station.

They heard the echo of the doorbell one more time, without any movement inside. Hanne Wilhelmsen stepped onto the small patch of grass separating the wall of the building from the sidewalk, standing on tiptoe and stretching up to the shaded window. Nothing stirred inside. She gave up and made a sign that the two others should return to their car. Once seated, Kaldbakken lit a cigarette while waiting restlessly for an explanation. Slipping into the rear seat, Hanne Wilhelmsen leaned forward to her two colleagues, supporting her elbows on the front seats and resting her head on her folded hands.

"What's this all about, Wilhelmsen?" Kaldbakken asked in an indescribably weary voice from the front.

It suddenly dawned on her she needed more time.

"I'll explain it all later," she said. "Tomorrow, maybe. Yes, definitely. Tomorrow."

He knew who it was going to be this Saturday. Today he had made up his mind. She claimed to be from Afghanistan, but he knew for certain she was lying. Pakistani, he was sure, but prettier than they usually were.

He was in bed. Not at one side of the large double bed, but right in the middle so he could feel the join in the mattress hard against his spine. The quilts were on the floor, and he was naked. In his hands he held dumbbells, slowly and regularly pulling them as far apart as possible, and then letting them crash together on outstretched arms above his perspiring rib cage.

"Ninety-one, *puff.* Ninety-two, *puff.*"

He felt happier than he had in a long time. At ease, free, full of strength.

He knew exactly whom he was going to lay his hands on. He knew exactly where he was going to do it. He also knew precisely what he was going to do.

Reaching one hundred, he heaved himself up into a sitting position. The massive wall mirror opposite showed him what he wanted to see. Then he headed for the shower.

For some reason, the idea of going home was not appealing. Hanne Wilhelmsen sat on a bench outside the police station at Grønlandsleiret 44, pondering life. She was exhausted, but not sleepy. Earlier it had been so clear to her there was some kind of connection between the Saturday night massacres and the rape of the sweet young medical student. But nothing was clear any longer.

She felt powerless to move from the spot. Their work of plotting and directing, sending troops here and there, in many ways felt effective. However, very little had come of it. The investigation was so technical. They were searching for hairs, fibers, and other specific clues. Every last drop of spittle was examined, and they received incomprehensible results from experts about DNA structures and blood types. Naturally, all that was necessary, but it was miles from being adequate. The Saturday man was not normal. In some ways there was intelligence behind his actions, a kind of absurd logic. He kept to a particular day of the week. If the hypothesis was true, that there were another three foreign women buried somewhere out there, then he was also rather smart. At the same time, he had chosen to put them on his trail by obliquely telling them whom he had mutilated.

Hanne Wilhelmsen had — in sharp contrast to the majority of her colleagues — some sort of respect for psychologists. She agreed that they spoke a lot of nonsense, but some of it made sense. It was obviously a branch of science, if not so terribly exact. On several occasions, she had ridden roughshod over opposition to procure psychological profiles of unidentified criminals. She didn't need that this time. As she leaned back on the bench, observing that it was now almost completely dark, it struck her that the harsh reality out there, in Europe, in the world, had long impacted criminality in Norway. They just didn't want to acknowledge it. It was too frightening. Twenty years earlier, serial murderers belonged in America. For the past decade, people had been able to read about similar cases in England.

There were not many mass murderers in Norwegian legal history. The few who existed had crazy and sad histories. Colleagues in Halden had recently arrested one of them. Chance murders presumably committed by the same man, over a long period of time, apparently without any motive other than cash. Some years before, a young man had killed three people he lived with in a commune in Slemdal, because they had reminded him about thirty thousand kroner he owed in rent. The expert forensic psychiatrist had concluded that he was definitely not insane.

What was the Saturday man's motive? She could only guess at that. From the textbooks she knew that criminals could possess a

225

more or less subconscious desire to be caught.

Hanne Wilhelmsen knew this was not the case here.

"He's enjoying poking fun at us," she whispered.

"Are you sitting here talking to yourself, now?"

She jumped out of her skin where she sat.

Billy T. stood facing her.

She stared at him momentarily in alarm and then laughed out loud.

"I must be getting old."

"I'll leave you in peace to grow old," Billy T. said, mounting his motorcycle, an enormous Honda Goldwing.

"I can't understand how you can be bothered driving around on that big bus of yours." She grinned before he managed to put on his helmet.

Looking derisively at her, he did not take the trouble to reply.

Suddenly she stood up and rushed to him as he was starting the engine. He couldn't hear what she was saying and had to remove his helmet.

"Are you going home?" she asked with no further thought.

"Yes, don't have too many alternatives at

this time of night," he said, glancing at his watch.

"Shall we go for a ride?"

"Can your Harley bear to be seen in the company of a Japanese?"

They drove around in the summer night for more than an hour. Hanne in front, making a deafening racket, and Billy T. following with a silky-soft, deep rumbling noise between his legs. They drove along the old Mossevei to Tyrigrava, and back again. Cruising along the city streets, they raised their hands in an obligatory wave to all the cowboys in leather gear beside the Tanum bookstore on Karl Johans gate, where the motorbikes were parked side by side, like horses tethered outside an old saloon.

They finished up right beside Tryvann Lake, at a huge parking lot without a single car, where they halted and parked their bikes.

"You can say many strange things about this spring weather of ours," Billy T. said, "but you can't say it's not good for biking!"

Oslo lay spread out before them. Dirty and dusty, with a lid of pollution clearly visible even though night had fallen. The sky wasn't completely dark and would probably not be so until the end of August. Here and there a faint star was twinkling. The others had tumbled down to earth. The entire city was a carpet with little lights springing up, from Gjelleråsen in the east to Bærum in the west. The sea lay black as pitch on the horizon.

At the edge of the parking lot there was a red-and-white road barrier, where it sloped down to a thicket of trees. Billy T. sauntered across and sat there, legs sprawling, and called her over.

"Come here now," he said, pulling her toward him.

She stood between his legs with her back leaning against his rib cage.

Reluctantly, she allowed herself to be held. He was so tall that their heads were side by side, though he was almost sitting and she was standing practically upright. He embraced her with his gigantic arms and moved his head closer to hers. With a certain feeling of surprise, she felt herself relax.

"Do you sometimes get fed up being a police officer, Hanne?" he asked quietly.

She nodded. They all became tired of it now and again. More and more frequently, to tell the truth.

"Look at that city there," he continued. "How many crimes do you think are taking place now? Right at this moment?"

Neither of them uttered a word.

"And here we stand, unable to do a thing," he added after a lengthy pause.

"It's amazing people don't protest," Hanne said.

"But they do," Billy T. replied. "They protest all the bloody time. We're hung out to dry every fucking day, in the newspapers, at lunch breaks all over the place, at parties. We're not held in very high regard, I can tell you that. I know them well. It's scary when they aren't satisfied with just complaining."

It really was pleasant, standing like this. He had a scent of maleness and leather, and his beard tickled her cheek. Taking hold of his arms, she tucked them more comfortably around her.

"Why do you keep up this show of secrecy, Hanne?" he said softly, almost whispering.

When he felt her freeze instantaneously and prepare to pull away, he was ready and held her tight.

"Don't mess about, listen to me now. Everybody knows you're a fantastic policewoman. Shit, there's hardly a damn policeman with your reputation. What's more, everyone likes you. They say good things about you everywhere."

She was still trying to shake herself free.

229

Then she realized that she at least avoided having eye contact by standing like this. And so she tolerated it, though it was far from comfortable.

"I've often wondered whether you know about the rumors circulating. Because they do circulate, you know. Maybe not as frequently as before, but people speculate, you can understand that. A lovely lady like you and never any gentleman friends."

She could sense he was smiling, though her gaze was firmly fixed on a point far off on the slopes of Ekebergåsen.

"It must be a drag, Hanne. A damnable drag."

His mouth was so close to her ear she could feel his lips move.

"All I wanted to say to you was, people are not as crazy as you think. There's a bit of tittle-tattle, and then it passes. When something is confirmed, it's not so interesting anymore. You're a great girl. Nothing changes that. I think you should put an end to all this show of secrecy."

Then he released her, but she didn't dare to move. Rooted to the spot, she remained standing there, absolutely terrified he might see her face. She was burning like embers and hardly dared to breathe.

Since she made no move to leave, he

embraced her again and began to rock her slowly from side to side. They stood like that for the eternity of a few seconds, while one light after another was extinguished in the city below.

TUESDAY, JUNE 8

No one was drinking coffee any longer; they were all drinking cola. Just the thought of letting a hot drink run down their dry throats was repellent. A beer stall in the foyer would have been a gold mine. The little refrigerator in the lunchroom emitted unhappy moans and sighs at all the plastic bottles stacked inside, unable even to chill before being taken out again.

That morning, Hanne Wilhelmsen had introduced iced tea to the staff of Section A 2.11. At seven o'clock, without a single hour's sleep, she went around scouring out all the ingrained dirt on the coffee machines. She then made fourteen liters in total of extremely strong tea, mixing it with heaps of sugar and two whole bottles of lemon essence, in an enormous steel home brew container "borrowed" from the room where confiscated items were stored. Finally, she filled the pot to the brim with crushed ice begged from the canteen. It was a great success. For the rest of the day, they all walked about with canteen tumblers brimful, slurping down iced tea, amazed no one had thought of this before.

"Thank God I've checked all these out." Erik Henriksen sighed in relief as he handed Hanne Wilhelmsen a bundle containing twelve tips about the Kristine Håverstad case.

It was the group containing lawyers and police. The one they had laughed at. The one she thank God had asked him to take care of. It took a quarter of an hour to read them all.

One tip-off stood out from the others and was repeated twice: "The artist's impression in *Dagbladet* on June first has a certain resemblance to Cato Iversen. His face is slightly thinner, but on the other hand he has been behaving oddly for a while now. As I work beside him, I'd prefer to remain anonymous. We both work in the Immigration Directorate, where he can be reached during normal office hours."

"Bull's-eye," Hanne Wilhelmsen mumbled, grabbing the other sheet of paper Erik expectantly handed her.

"I was struck by how much the sketch looked like my neighbor Cato Iversen," the

233

tip said. "He lives at Ulveveien 3, Kolsås, and works in the Immigration Directorate, as far as I know. He has been away from home at various times. He is unmarried."

The letter was signed, accompanied by a robust request to allow the name anonymity.

Thirty seconds later, Hanne Wilhelmsen was standing in Håkon Sand's office.

"I need a blue sheet."

"For which case?"

"This case. Look here."

She gave him both reports, but his reaction was quite different from what she expected. Calmly, he read them through a couple of times before returning them.

"Now you must listen to my theory," she began, slightly confused by the attorney's devastating composure. "Have you heard about signature crimes?"

Of course he had, he read the textbooks as well.

"The murderer leaves behind some kind of trademark, doesn't he? The mark becomes known, through the newspapers or as the subject of gossip. Then there's somebody who wants to get rid of somebody else, and who therefore disguises 'his' . . ."

She waved her fingers in the air.

". . . 'his' murder as one of the original series."

"But it never goes well," Håkon Sand muttered.

"No, exactly. As a rule it goes awry because the police, naturally, have not released all the details of the trademark. But here, Håkon, here we have precisely the opposite situation."

"The opposite situation. Oh, yes. Of what, then?"

"Of the murder that's sneaked in, disguised as one of a series."

Håkon Sand coughed discreetly into his clenched fist, hoping she would provide a further explanation without needing too much encouragement.

"Here we have a signature killer making a slip! He's going to commit another murder in the series, but then something goes wrong. No, let me be quite specific."

Drawing the chair over to his desk, she grabbed a blank sheet of paper and a pen, and quickly outlined a miniature copy of the time line on the flip chart in the operations room.

"On May twenty-ninth, he goes out to rape and murder an asylum seeker. This asylum seeker."

She slapped a case folder onto the desk.

Håkon didn't touch it but inclined his head to see the name on the cover. It was the woman on the floor below. The one they had tried to contact the previous evening.

"Look here," Hanne said, almost too eagerly, leafing through the documents. "She's absolutely perfect. Came to Norway on her own. To meet her father, she thought, but he died a few days before her arrival. Then she inherited the apartment and some money, and has been living quietly in the expectation they'll get the finger out at the Immigration Directorate. A perfect victim. Doesn't even live at a reception center."

"But why didn't he take her, then, if she was so perfect?"

"We don't know that, of course. But my hypothesis is that she was away. Out, gone, whatever. She told me she'd been sleeping and hadn't heard anything, but she looked terrified of the police, the way these people do, so it might just as well have been a lie. But then he's standing there, until Kristine Håverstad turns up. Snazzy girl. Very attractive. Then he simply makes a swap."

Håkon Sand had to admit that something about her theory did hold water.

"But why didn't he kill her then?"

"That's obvious," Hanne Wilhelmsen responded, getting to her feet. She appeared stiff and tired, despite her enthusiasm. Arms akimbo, her upper body swaying several times from side to side.

"How many cases of rape do we drop, Håkon?"

He flung his arms out wide. "No idea. But it's a helluva lot. Far too many."

Returning to her seat, she leaned toward him. The scar above her eye looked more prominent now, he noticed. Had she lost weight?

"We drop more than a hundred rape cases every year, Håkon. More than a hundred! How many of them do you think we've investigated thoroughly?"

"Not so many," he mumbled, rather conscience stricken. He instinctively glanced in the direction of a bundle containing three cases ready and waiting for the "dismissed" stamp. Rapes. All of them slim files. Virtually zero investigation.

"How many murder cases do we drop every year?" she asked rhetorically.

"We hardly ever drop murder cases!"

"Exactly! He *could not* kill Kristine Håverstad. It would have been discovered a few hours later, and we would have been like wasps buzzing around the city. This guy is smart."

She hit the desktop with her fist.

"Damn smart!"

"But he hasn't been so bloody smart, you know. He let Kristine see his face, didn't he?"

"Only just, yes. And look at what kind of drawing that gave us. Not very specific."

They were interrupted by a female assistant police attorney entering to hand him a remand-in-custody file.

"There's another five of those coming from Larceny," she said sympathetically before disappearing out the door.

"All the same, there's one thing I can't get to add up," Håkon said reflectively. "If he's got this perfect arrangement, why doesn't he stick to it? He surely can't have been so sexually pumped up he just *had* to have someone?"

Of course he might have been. Hanne Wilhelmsen and Håkon Sand both thought of it in the same split second. The previous spring, Oslo had seen a string of rapes; in fact, those too were mostly in the Homansbyen area. The rapist had finally been caught, by sheer chance. The explanation for why he had done it struck them both simultaneously.

"Roids," Håkon Sand exclaimed, looking at his colleague, almost afraid. "Anabolic steroids!"

238

"We're looking for a muscleman," Hanne Wilhelmsen said drily. "Still more clues. And right now, as I said, I'd like a blue sheet for this guy here. He looks perfect."

She thumped her fingers down on the two reports she had brought and placed a blue form before him. He let them lie.

"You're exhausted now," he said.

"Exhausted? Yes, of course I'm exhausted."

"You're so exhausted you're not thinking clearly."

"Thinking clearly? What on earth do you mean by that?"

Obviously she was tired. They all were. But it didn't help matters that Håkon Sand was trying to delay an extremely welcome arrest.

"There's not enough there to warrant an arrest," he declared, folding his arms across his chest. "You know that very well."

Hanne Wilhelmsen did not quite know what to believe. It had been many years since a police lawyer had denied her an arrest decision. She had never, not once in the four years they had been working together, been refused one by Håkon Sand. Her surprise was so great it almost displaced her rapidly escalating anger.

"Do you really mean . . ."

She stood up, supporting herself by the desk in a vaguely threatening pose.

"Are you telling me you're refusing to fill out a blue sheet?"

He simply nodded.

"But what the h—"

She lifted her eyes skyward, as though someone up there could offer assistance.

"What on earth do you mean by that?"

"I mean that what you've got there is nowhere near enough to justify an arrest. Bring the guy in as we usually do. See if you can get anything out of him. Then we can discuss it. With a view to custody, possibly."

"Custody? I'm not bloody asking for him to be remanded in custody! I'm asking for a normal, simple blue sheet in an insane case that may have cost four girls their lives!"

Håkon Sand had never seen Hanne Wilhelmsen so furious. Nonetheless, he stood his ground. He knew he was right. Two tip-offs about a possible killer were not sufficient grounds for suspicion. Even though he worked in the Immigration Directorate and so had open access to all the information his heart desired about asylum seekers. He shuddered at the thought.

It was not enough. He knew that. And he knew Hanne Wilhelmsen actually knew it too. Perhaps that was why he said nothing more. Clutching both the uncompleted blue sheet and the two reports, she slammed the door hard behind her as she left.

"Shit bag," she muttered as she walked along the corridor.

A weary chap sitting in an uncomfortable chair waiting his turn for some interrogation or other obviously felt offended and stared uneasily at the floor.

"Not you," she added, marching on.

Erik Henriksen was sitting in the office, waiting eagerly. He received no explanation, only an overpolite demand — for crying out loud — to get hold of Kristine Håverstad. They needed her. Now. Right away. An hour since. He rushed off.

She looked in the phone catalog to find the Immigration Directorate's number. After breathing deeply five times to calm herself down properly, she dialed the number.

"Cato Iversen, please," she requested.

"He's on telephone duty between ten and two. You have to phone back then," replied the dry, flat voice.

"I'm phoning from the police. I need to talk to Iversen. Now."

"What was the name?"

The lady didn't give up easily.

"Hanne Wilhelmsen. Oslo police station."

"One moment, please."

That was a real understatement. After four minutes of deafening silence, without as much as a little peep of "You are still in the queue, please wait," she angrily pressed the button to terminate the call and redialed the number.

"Immigration Directorate, go ahead."

It was the same woman.

"This is Hanne Wilhelmsen, Murder, Manslaughter, and Rape Department, Oslo Police. I want to speak to Cato Iversen immediately."

The woman was evidently seriously alarmed by the new name given to the Homicide Section. Ten seconds later, Cato Iversen was on the line. He introduced himself by his surname.

"Good morning," Hanne said in as noncommittal a tone as she could manage in present circumstances. "This is Hanne Wilhelmsen, Homicide Section, Oslo Police, here."

"Yes," the man said, without a trace of anxiety, as far as Hanne could discern. She quickly comforted herself that he was probably well used to talking to the police.

"I'd like to conduct an interview with you in connection with a case we're investigating. It's fairly urgent. Can you manage to come in?"

"Now? Right away?"

"Yes, as soon as possible."

The man took some time to think. There was a silence, at least.

"That's impossible at the moment. I'm sorry. But I . . ."

She could hear him leafing through papers. He seemed to be checking his appointments diary.

"I can manage to come next Monday."

"That's unfortunately not suitable. I need to speak to you now. It probably won't take long." Which was a downright lie.

"What's it about?"

"We can talk about that when you get here. I'll be expecting you in an hour."

"No, honestly. It's just not possible. I'm giving a lecture at an internal training session we're running now."

"I suggest you come here immediately," Hanne said quietly. "Say you are sick, say whatever you want. I can of course come and pick you up. But perhaps you'd rather get here under your own steam."

Now the man was clearly nervous. But who wouldn't have been after such an exchange? Hanne thought, choosing not to place too much emphasis on the alteration in the man's demeanor.

"I can be there in half an hour," he said finally. "Perhaps slightly longer. But I'm on my way."

Kristine Håverstad did not know what to do. Her father had left for work as usual at eight o'clock. She was no longer sure, however, that this was what he was actually doing. In order to confirm her suspicions, she phoned the dentist's surgery and asked to speak to her father.

"But my dear girl, Kristine," the buxom, matronly receptionist answered. "Your father's on vacation! Didn't you know?"

Kristine did her best to persuade the lady it was all down to a misunderstanding and replaced the receiver. She had no doubt that her father intended to carry out his plan. They had talked for more than an hour last evening, at greater length than they had done during all of the previous ten days.

The worst part was that it all seemed liberating. It was grotesque, terrifying, insane. People didn't do that sort of thing. Not here in this country, at least. But the thought that the man would die nevertheless caused her to feel relieved. She experienced a kind of elation at the possibility of some sort of reparation. He had destroyed two lives. He deserved no better. At least not when the police evidently weren't doing anything at all to capture him. And even if they did manage to do so, he would probably receive a year in a fancy cell with TV and leisure activities. He wasn't worth that.

He deserved to die. She hadn't deserved what he had done to her. He was a thief and a murderer. Her father didn't deserve what he had to endure. Once she had more or less calmed down into some sense of quiet satisfaction that a decision had been made, she froze. This was madness, pure and simple. You didn't just kill other people. But if anyone was going to do it, she had to be the one.

It had been ages since Billy T. had been an investigator. He had been in the surveillance team of the drug squad for more than five years. So long that he would probably remain a cop in denims until he became too old for it. However, his skills as an interrogator were still legendary. He didn't always play it by the book, but he'd achieved a number of confessions that impressed the best of them. Hanne Wilhelmsen had insisted, and he had allowed himself to be persuaded. It dawned on her it might all be a ruse to see him again. The previous night seemed totally unreal, now that she was back in secure surroundings with all her usual defenses in place. Nevertheless, she had a strong urge to see him, talk to him, about everyday things, police business. She simply wanted to reassure herself he was still the same old guy.

It was him. He made a lot of noise, cracking jokes, all the way to her office — she could hear him before she saw him. When he caught sight of her, as she popped her head out the door to greet him, he called out flirtatious remarks without a scintilla of a hint about what had occurred only a few hours earlier. He did not appear particularly tired either. Everything was as it had been. Nearly, at least.

When Hanne Wilhelmsen clapped eyes on Cato Iversen, it gave her a shock. Perhaps he didn't look so very like the artist's impression, but he perfectly matched the description Kristine Håverstad had given. Broad shoulders, blond hair receding on both sides. Not conspicuously tall, but his muscular body made a fairly pronounced impression all the same. He was tanned as well, but on the other hand, most people were now. Except the police officers in Oslo police station.

Billy T. on his own virtually filled the

room. With the addition of Cato Iversen and Hanne Wilhelmsen, it was really crowded. Billy T. positioned himself with his back to the window, his backside resting on the sill. Against the harsh daylight he became an enormous black figure with sharp edges and no face. Hanne Wilhelmsen sat in her usual place.

Cato Iversen looked noticeably nervous. Still, this was not itself unusual and did not indicate anything untoward. Swallowing nonstop, he sat restlessly in his chair and displayed a peculiar bad habit of perpetually scratching the back of his left hand.

"As you may know," she began, "we don't usually use a tape recorder during witness interviews."

He did not know that.

"But we're doing so in this case," she continued, smiling easily, and simultaneously pressing two buttons on a small tape recorder on the desk. She adjusted the microphone so that it pointed at random into the room.

"We'll start with your personal details," she declared.

She was given these and reciprocated by informing him he did not need to give a statement but should tell the truth if he chose to say anything.

"Am I entitled to a lawyer?"

He regretted it as soon as he had spoken and attempted to take it back by smiling faintly, shaking his head deprecatingly, and clearing his throat. He clawed feverishly at an imaginary mosquito bite on his left hand.

"A lawyer, Billy T.," Hanne said, directing her comment to the monster on the windowsill. "A lawyer? Does our friend here need an attorney?"

Billy T. said nothing, only smiled. Iversen could not see that. From where he was sitting, the man was still only a black outline against the bright blue sky.

"No, no, I don't need one. It was just a question."

"You're a witness, Iversen," Hanne Wilhelmsen assured him in an exaggerated effort to mollify the man. "You don't need an attorney, then?"

"But what's all this about?"

"We'll come to that, we'll come to that."

A siren screamed its way down Åkebergveien at lightning speed, immediately followed by another.

"A lot to do in this weather," Hanne explained. "Where is it you work?"

"At the Immigration Directorate."

"What do you do there?"

"I'm an administrator. Just an ordinary

administrator."

"Oh, yes, and what does an ordinary administrator do?"

"Administers cases."

It was obviously not the man's intention to appear impertinent, as after a short pause he added, "I take in the applications for residence permission the police have already dealt with. We are the initial decision-making authority."

"Asylum cases?"

"Both that and others. Reuniting families. Study visits. I deal only with cases from Asia."

"Do you like your job?"

"Like?"

"Yes, do you find it enjoyable work?"

"Yes and no."

He thought about it.

"It's a job like any other, I suppose. I qualified as a lawyer last year. You can't always pick and choose. The job's okay, as far as it goes."

"It's not sad, then, throwing out all these poor souls?"

Now he seemed genuinely taken aback. He had not exactly expected such an attitude from the police.

"Not sad," he mumbled. "It's Parliament that decides. We just carry out the decisions they have made. What's more, not all of them are thrown out, you know."

"But most of them, isn't that so?"

"Well, yes, perhaps the majority."

"What's your opinion of foreigners, then?"

Now he had obviously recovered slightly.

"Honestly," he said, changing his position in the chair. "Now I really need to know what this is all about."

The two police officers exchanged glances, and Billy T. nodded briefly. Iversen could see that too.

"We're toiling with a fairly serious case at the moment," Hanne Wilhelmsen told him. "The Saturday night massacres. You've probably read about them?"

He had indeed. He nodded and began to scratch himself again.

"In each of the pools of blood, we found a number. An immigration number. On Sunday we found a body. A body that looks to be from Asia. And do you know what?"

Seeming almost enthusiastic, she rummaged until she found a sheet of paper in the bundle in front of her.

"Two of these immigration numbers are from cases you're dealing with!"

The man's nervousness had increased, and now they could possibly begin to read something into it.

"There aren't so very many of us who work on the cases from Asia," he interjected rapidly. "It's not strange in the least."

"No, I see."

"I mean, you have to know how many cases we handle every year. Several hundred each. Maybe several thousand," he added quickly, obviously in an effort to strengthen his argument.

"Perhaps you'll be able to help me, then, since you have such a lot of experience. How do you deal with these cases, actually? I mean, like, from an administrative point of view. Is it all on computers?"

"Yes, all the data is entered into the computers, that's right. But we have files as well, of course. With papers, I mean. Interview reports and letters and that kind of thing."

"And they contain all the details of each individual asylum seeker?"

"Yes. Well, yes, all we need to know, at least."

"Such things as who they came with, family relationships, whether they know anybody here, why they came to Norway in particular, all of that kind of thing. Is that contained in your files?"

The man squirmed in his seat again and seemed to be considering this.

251

"Yes, that's all in the police interview reports."

Hanne Wilhelmsen knew that. She had spent an hour reading the police interview reports on the four women that same morning.

"Are there many who arrive all on their own?"

"A few. Others have their family with them. Some have family here already."

"Some of them disappear, I've heard?"

"Disappear?"

"Yes, they vanish out of the system without anyone knowing where they are."

"Oh, yes, that kind of disappear . . . Yes, that happens now and again."

"What do you do with them, then?"

"Nothing."

Now Billy T. moved his colossal frame from the window ledge. His backside was cold after sitting on the dilapidated fresh air system for twenty minutes. Maneuvering himself around Hanne Wilhelmsen, he came to a stop with his arm leaning against a shiny bookshelf, as he peered down at the witness.

"Now we'll get straight to the point, Iversen," he said. "Where do you usually hang out on the weekends?"

The man did not respond. The scratching

was now pronounced.

"Stop that," Hanne Wilhelmsen ordered, irritated.

Though Cato Iversen was becoming desperate, it barely registered. The two police officers studied him intently but still could not see anything other than a touch of nervousness. Iversen had no idea what to say. Therefore he blurted out the truth.

"I drive a pickup," he said softly.

Billy T. and Hanne exchanged looks, and both smiled.

"You drive a pickup," Hanne repeated slowly.

"Did you drive your pickup on Saturday, May twenty-ninth, too? What about Sunday the thirtieth?"

Bloody hell. They had him. All the other stuff was simply window dressing. Despite Hanne Wilhelmsen's outburst a minute earlier, he was scratching his left hand desperately. It had become painful, so he stopped.

"I want to speak to an attorney," he exclaimed suddenly. "I'm saying nothing further until I get to speak to an attorney."

"But my dear man, Iversen," Billy T. said smooth as silk, crouching down in front of him. "You aren't accused of anything."

"But I'm suspected of something," Iversen

replied, and now they could see he had tears in his eyes. "And so I need an attorney."

Leaning across her desk, Hanne switched off the tape recorder.

"Iversen. Let one thing be crystal clear. We are interviewing you now as a witness. You do not have the status of either a suspect or an accused. Ergo you have no need of an attorney. Ergo you have the right to walk out of this room and out of this building whenever you like. If you nevertheless choose to have a chat with an attorney, and have another conversation with us afterward, you are of course free to do so."

She grabbed the telephone and placed it directly in front of him. Then she slapped the Yellow Pages beside it.

"Go ahead," she invited him, checking quickly around the little office to see whether there was anything he should not access. She grasped a bundle of case files and, taking Billy T. with her, headed for the door, where she paused.

"We'll be back in ten minutes," she said.

It turned out to be rather more than a mere ten minutes. They sat in the operations room, each with a glass of Hanne's morning brew. The ice had melted, the sugar had sunk to the bottom of the nearly depleted container, and with the tannin the drink was not nearly as refreshing as it had been several hours earlier.

"Now he'll haul himself in," Billy T. said. "We didn't need to say very much."

"Your appearance alone can frighten the most innocent of people into confessing anything at all." Hanne grinned, draining her glass. "What's more, I don't know if he's quite ready to be pulled in."

"Something's making him quake, that's for sure," Billy T. remarked. "That's my opinion. But I've got to go. I'm wiped. You probably are too," he added, attempting to make eye contact.

She did not respond and simply raised her empty glass in a hollow toast as he left the room, to be replaced by Erik Henriksen storming in.

"I found her," he puffed. "She was actually on her way here! She was standing right in the doorway! What were you wanting her for?"

It took only an hour and a half to organize a face-to-face. There appeared to be a surprising number of broad-shouldered, blond men with receding hairlines in the police. Five of them were now standing in company with Cato Iversen in the identity parade room. On the other side of a one-way glass window, Kristine Håverstad stood biting her nails.

This was not why she had come, of course. She had almost collided with the freckled police officer as she diffidently approached the police station. She still had time to retreat from her purpose when he, beaming with pleasure, had confirmed her identity and brought her inside. Luckily, she hadn't needed to say anything at all.

Detective Inspector Hanne Wilhelmsen appeared far more exhausted than she had barely a week prior. Her eyes seemed paler, her mouth tighter and more determined. The previous week, Kristine Håverstad had thought her strikingly beautiful. Now she was an ordinary woman with attractive features, wearing no makeup. She did not seem terribly enthusiastic either, though she was friendly and welcoming enough.

The six men followed one another into the room, like a flock of well-fed geese. When the first had reached the far end of the floor, they all turned to stare blindly into the windowpane. Kristine knew they could not see her.

He wasn't there. They all looked alike. But none of them was the man who had attacked her. She felt tears well up. If only . . .

if only it had been one of them. Then he would have been safe from her father. She could attempt to patch up her life again. She would be spared from warning the police that her own father was planning to commit a murder. Life would have been so totally different if it had only been one of them. But it wasn't.

"Perhaps number two," she blurted out.

What was she doing? It was definitely not number two. But by forcing them to hold one of them, she would be able to buy herself some time at least. Some time to think, some time to dissuade her father. A few days, perhaps, but something was always better than nothing.

"Or number three?"

She looked questioningly at Hanne Wilhelmsen, who however was sitting like a sphinx, looking directly ahead.

"Yes," she decided. "Number two or number three. But I'm not at all sure."

Detective Inspector Hanne Wilhelmsen thanked her for her assistance, ushered her out, and was so disappointed she forgot to ask Kristine Håverstad what her original errand had been. It did not matter. Slinging her bag across a narrow shoulder, Kristine Håverstad disappeared from the police station, in the sure knowledge she would never have been able to bring herself to tell tales on her father.

Number two in the lineup was office worker Fredrik Andersen of the Subpoena section.

Number three was Police Sergeant Eirik Langbråtan, a pleasant fellow who was a crime desk operator. Cato Iversen, who had been number six in the row, received a handshake, a lackluster apology, and permission to leave.

Having reached the far end of Grønlandsleiret and out of sight of anyone watching him from the enormous curved building, Iversen entered the Lompa restaurant, where he bought himself two liters of beer all at once. Sitting down at a table tucked inside the premises, he lit a cigarette with trembling hands.

On the night of May 29, he had been on board the Danish ferry with a pickup loaded with smuggled liquor. That would never, ever happen again.

Virtually an entire working day had been wasted on a dead end. It was nothing less than disheartening. But this would not turn out to be the most dominant event in A 2.11 that day.

Chief Inspector Hans Olav Kaldbakken

entered Hanne Wilhelmsen's office for his daily briefing. He did not look good at all. Sitting down in the chair with stiff, labored movements, he lit himself a cigarette, his twentieth that day, though it was not yet half past three.

"Are we getting anywhere, Wilhelmsen?" he inquired hoarsely. "Have we anything else to go on apart from this . . . this Cato Iversen? For it can't be him, can it?"

"No, it can't be, true enough," Hanne Wilhelmsen answered, massaging her temples.

The confirmation was a considerable understatement. Cato Iversen possibly had his own skeleton in the cupboard, but that would have to wait for another day. Hanne had a gut feeling Kristine Håverstad would have recognized her assailant. It puzzled her why the young woman had picked out two people who so evidently had not done her any harm. It may have been a deeply subconscious desire to give them something. But it had been worthy of note. She'd have to think about it another time.

"Saturday is approaching," Kaldbakken said ponderously. "It's getting terribly close to Saturday."

He had a peculiar dialect and swallowed his words before they were completely enunciated. But Hanne Wilhelmsen had worked with the same boss for many years and always understood what he meant.

"It is indeed, Kaldbakken. It's getting near to Saturday."

"Do you know something," he said, leaning toward her in an unusual display of familiarity. "Rapes are the worst things I know. I just can't stand rapes. And I've been a policeman now for thirty years."

He was momentarily lost in thought but quickly pulled himself together.

"For thirty-three years, to be precise. I started in 1960, which doesn't exactly make me an old man."

Giving a stern smile, he coughed violently.

"The sixties. Those were the days. It was good to be a policeman then. Well paid, so we were. More than industrial workers. Quite a lot more. People had respect for us in those times. Gerhardsen was still prime minister, and people were all pulling in the same direction."

The smoke was already clogging the room. The man rolled his own cigarettes and was spitting tobacco in between his soft-spoken mumblings.

"At that time we had about two or three rapes a year. Terrible commotion. We usually got the bastard too. It was mostly men here then, and rapes were the worst crimes we knew. All of us. We didn't give up until we'd caught them."

Hanne Wilhelmsen had never experienced this. She had worked with the chief inspector for seven years and had never talked about anything more intimate than an upset stomach. For some reason, she took this as a bad sign.

Kaldbakken sighed deeply, and she could hear the gurgling in his overexerted bronchial tubes.

"But on the whole it's been good being in the police," he commented, gazing dreamily into space. "When you go to bed at night, you know you're one of the good guys.

"And girls," he added with a cautious smile. "It gives a meaning to your existence. At least it has up till now. After this spring, I don't know, to tell the truth."

Hanne Wilhelmsen well understood him. It had really been a dreadful year. For her, despite everything, things were going fairly easily. She was thirty-four years old, only just born when Kaldbakken, stiff and straight in his newly pressed uniform, had been patrolling along the long, quiet streets of Oslo. She had a lot going for her. Kaldbakken did not. She came around to wondering how old he was. He looked well over sixty, but that couldn't be right. He had to be younger than that.

"I haven't got much left to give, Hanne," he mumbled.

It scared her that he called her Hanne. Until today she had never been anything other than Wilhelmsen to him.

"That's nonsense, Kaldbakken," she ventured, but gave up when he brushed her aside.

"I know when it's time to give in. I —"

A terrifying, violent paroxysm of coughing suddenly gripped him. It lasted for a disturbing length of time. Finally, Hanne Wilhelmsen stood up uncertainly and placed her hand on his back.

"Can I help you? Do you want a glass of water or something?"

When he leaned back in the chair, gasping for breath, she became seriously alarmed. His face was gray and pouring with sweat. Moving to the side, he struggled for air and then fell heavily. There was an awful crunching sound as he hit the floor.

Standing with her feet apart above the crumpled body, Hanne Wilhelmsen managed to turn him around and shout for help.

When there was no response after two seconds, she kicked the door open and shouted again.

"Call for an ambulance, for God's sake!

Phone for a doctor!"

She then set in with mouth-to-mouth resuscitation on her old, worn-out boss. Two breaths, then heart massage. Two breaths, and heart massage again. There was a snapping sound inside his chest, and she realized she had broken some ribs.

Erik Henriksen was standing in the doorway, bewildered and redder than ever.

"Heart massage," she commanded, concentrating her efforts on his breathing.

The young lad squeezed and squeezed. Hanne Wilhelmsen blew and blew. But when the paramedics stood at the door nine minutes later, Chief Inspector Hans Olav Kaldbakken was dead, at only fifty-six years of age.

In a drab, unattractive room in a boarding-house in Lillehammer, the little Iranian woman from Kristine Håverstad's block was sitting, brokenhearted. She was on her own, terribly far from home, with no one to ask for help. She had chosen Lillehammer completely by chance. Far enough away but not too expensive on the train. Moreover, she had heard of the folk museum at Maihaugen.

She should of course have spoken to the police. On the other hand, you couldn't always rely on them. She knew that from hard-earned experience. Quite intuitively, she had felt confidence in the young female officer who had spoken to her briefly the previous Monday. But what did she know, a little woman from Iran, about who could be trusted?

Taking out her Koran, she sat leafing through the pages. She read a little here and there but found no words of comfort or advice. After two hours, she fell asleep and did not wake until it struck her she had hardly eaten anything in two whole days.

As expected, her boss had been as cross as two sticks. She had apologized, promising him a doctor's note. Wherever she would get that from now. The emergency doctor, perhaps. At the Rape Crisis Center they had been friendly and courteous when she had gone there for the most humiliating examination imaginable the previous Sunday. All the same, she was reluctant to go there and ask. Well, she'd have to deal with that problem later. Grumpy and dismissive, her boss had muttered something about the youth of today. Kristine couldn't be bothered being provoked. She had never been out sick before.

"Kristine!"

Radiant with happiness, one of them grabbed hold of her. It was unbelievable that he was eighty-one years old. Unbelievable, since he had been in the navy for five years during the war and after that an alcoholic for almost fifty. But he stood his ground, in obstinate protest against the lack of recognition afforded to him and his long-dead shipmates.

"Kristine, my lass!"

She managed to break free after a quarter of an hour. She had not chosen the time of day at random. It was the change of shift, and she was able to sneak unseen into the storeroom where the medicine cabinet was situated. She wondered fleetingly whether she should lock the door. Then it dawned on her it would be more difficult to explain a locked rather than an open door. Although she shouldn't be in there, she could always come up with some plausible explanation or other. She fished out the keys to the medicine cupboard. They rattled too much, so she clutched the key ring and held her breath. What nonsense. With the hubbub in the corridor outside, there was little chance anyone would hear her. And what she was going to do would not take long either.

The packs of Nozinan were directly in front of her, in large quantities. She wondered whether she should choose injection or pill form. Without further thought, she grabbed the former. She didn't need syringes; she had some at home. Quick as a flash, she shut the cabinet behind her and crept over to the door. Holding her breath for thirty seconds, she stuffed the medication in her pocket and strolled nonchalantly out the door. There were only two clients in the corridor, and they were so inebriated they barely knew what day of the week it was.

On the way out, she reassured her boss once again that she would send a sick note, and that yes, of course, she would soon be back at work. Only a few days. He let her go with a sarcastic comment under his breath, which she could hear plainly.

It had gone well. The next part was more difficult.

It didn't seem as though she had been away for very long. Some nodded and smiled over their books, others stared blankly at her and buried themselves in their studies once more. Then she caught sight of Terje. He was sitting in the common room with five others she knew well, and she received a warmer welcome here. Especially from Terje. Four years her junior, he was a first-year student. Since the beginning of term, he had been clinging to her like a limpet. In umpteen different ways, he had declared his great love for her, paying hardly any attention to either the difference in their ages or the fact he was eight centimeters shorter. He was really sweet, and for the most part she took a kind of pleasure in his courtship.

"Persistence wins the day." He brushed her aside gallantly on the occasions when she, irritated, had felt that enough was enough and attempted to tell him the lay of the land.

She collapsed into a vacant chair.

"Heavens, what do you look like," commented one of her close friends. "You must've been really ill, I can see that!"

"Much better now." She smiled.

The others didn't look very convinced.

"And I'd really like to celebrate being back on my feet again. A little jaunt into town. Tomorrow. Wednesday night. Anyone want to come?"

They all did. Especially Terje. That was the point.

It had to happen on Wednesday. The best day. On Friday he would run a number of risks. The guy could be planning a weekend in the country. Or a party at home, for that matter. What's more, people stayed up late on Fridays. He needed peace and quiet, so it would have to take place on Wednesday evening. He could do it on Thursday but couldn't muster the patience. It had to be Wednesday.

Moreover, there was another important point about that day. He had told his daughter it would take place on Thursday. Now she would avoid having to wait. On Thursday morning he would waken her with the news it was all over.

The closet was locked, in accordance with the regulations. It was of course unnecessary now, since Kristine was grown up and did not touch his belongings. Indeed, she had hardly been inside his bedroom since she had been at high school.

Three Home Guard uniforms were hanging neatly in a row. With three stars on the epaulettes. He was a captain. Even the green field uniform was smoothly pressed. Two pairs of boots were lined up on the floor beneath the clothes. There was a faint smell of shoe cream and mothballs.

At the very back, behind both shoes and uniforms, lay a little steel case. Crouching down, he dragged it forward. Then, placing the case on the nightstand, he sat on the bed and opened it. The service pistol was made in Austria. Glock. Nine-millimeter ammunition. He had plenty of that. He could not touch his service ammo, but he had two broken boxes from the last shooting practice. To be persnickety, it was theft, but the top brass shut their eyes to it. It was so easy, of course, for boxes of ammunition to disappear underneath a car seat.

With unaccustomed fingers, he dismantled the gun, oiled it, and then dried it thoroughly with a rag. He placed the pistol by his side on the bed, wrapped in the polishing cloth. Then he took five cartridges from one of the boxes, replacing the remainder inside the steel case, locking it, returning the whole kit to the back of the closet and turning the key.

Stopping momentarily, he wondered where he should store his gun in the meantime. Finally he decided simply to stash it underneath the bed. The cleaning lady did not come until Friday, and by that time the weapon would be back in its rightful place.

He undressed and stepped into the bathroom adjacent to his bedroom. It took some time to fill the bathtub, so he threw on a dressing gown and went to mix a strong drink, although the afternoon was too young, strictly speaking. When he came back, the foam had reached almost the top of the bathtub rim, and it spilled over when he lowered himself into the scalding hot water.

Only yesterday had it really struck him that what he intended to do was a punishable offense. To put it mildly. The thought struck him like a hammer blow, for a split second, and then he pushed it away. He would not acknowledge it. Now he let the certainty that he was about to turn himself into a criminal sink more deeply.

It had never, not for a single moment, dawned on him that he could go to the police with what he knew. Actually, he was infuriated that they apparently were incapable of investigating as well as he had. It had all been frighteningly easy. It had taken him a few days. What were the police actually doing? Nothing? They had told him they had obtained fibers and traces of semen. For analysis. But what would they do with the results when they had no register to compare them? When he had asked the police officer that very question, she had shrugged her shoulders in resignation without giving an answer.

The police would have done something, right enough, if he went to them. He had no doubt about that. Probably the man would be arrested and subjected to tests of one kind or another. Then they would be able to prove it was him, and after that he would be put in prison. For a year or eighteen months. Minus a third of the sentence for good behavior. It meant the man could get away with less than a year behind bars. Less than a year! For having broken his daughter. Destroyed, humiliated, and defiled her.

Going to the police was out of the question. They would have to get on with their own business. Which was more than enough, if the newspaper headlines were anything to go by.

Naturally he could try to get away with it. Concoct an alibi of some kind. But he did not think much about that sort of thing. What's more, he wasn't interested.

Finn Håverstad was not concerned with getting away with the homicide he was planning of the man who had raped his daughter. He would ensure he managed to carry out his intention in peace. Then he would spend a few hours with Kristine, before giving himself up to the police and telling them what he had done. No one would condemn him for it. Of course he would be dealt his punishment, by a court of law, but no one would really condemn him. He would never have condemned himself. His friends would certainly not do so. And when all was said and done, when push came to shove, Finn Håverstad did not give a toss what others might say. It was essential for him to kill. It was justice.

The man Finn Håverstad lay in his bathtub planning to murder had changed his mind. Yesterday he had been so determined, so definite about doing it. Now he wanted to skip a Saturday. It did not matter a jot that they had found the body in the abandoned garden. He was one hundred percent certain nobody had been there for several years. That was possibly why he had been slightly slipshod with the depth. He had had too much to do. Bloody hell. It was good to get coverage in the newspapers, though. Perhaps that was what had blinded him yesterday. Now, after further thought, it struck him that things were becoming dangerous.

By a quirk of fate, he was sitting with a glass of exactly the same brand of whiskey as Håverstad the dentist had on the edge of his bath. It would break his pattern. That was what he enjoyed most. What had bothered the police most. He particularly liked the blood aspect. It aroused interest. If it had not been for that very detail, he would not have been given so much attention. And pigs' blood! On Muslims!

When the body was discovered, however, it immediately became more serious. Now he had to reckon on them allocating more resources. That was not his intention at all. It was a fucking nuisance they had found the body.

The lady was as round as a ball and deeply suspicious by nature. After forty years of running a boardinghouse, no one was going to come here and pull the wool over her eyes. It was one thing that they were going to have those Olympic Games here in the winter.

"We'll be well rid of those foreigners there," she mumbled to herself as she spread thick slices of bread with half a gram of butter, making it extend as far out toward the edges as possible. The thicker she cut the slices, the fuller the guests would be. Then they used up fewer sandwich toppings. Bread was cheaper than the cold meats and cheese. Simple arithmetic. She had calculated with satisfaction that she could save up to sixty or seventy kroner in only one round of supper. There was money to be made that way, in the long run.

"We'll get rid of those foreigners at the Olympics, oh, yes, but these asylum seekers, we're worse off with them," she continued grimly without anyone listening, apart from an enormous brindled cat that had jumped onto the kitchen worktop.

"Kitty, kitty, get yourself down from there!"

A couple of cat hairs had fallen onto one of the buttered slices, and she plucked them off with her small, plump fingers.

Then she came to a decision.

Drying her hands on her voluminous apron that was far from clean, she lifted the receiver on an old-fashioned black telephone with a rotary dial. Her fingers were so fat that she could not fit them properly into the holes, but she managed to dial the number for the police. She had it taped beside the telephone, handy should the occasion arise.

"Hello? This is Mrs. Brøttum from the Guesthouse! I want to report an illegal immigrant!"

Mrs. Brøttum managed to report her immigrant to a patient lady who assured her they would investigate the matter. After ten minutes oohing and aahing about all the Muslims flooding into the country, with their obvious special attraction to the Lillehammer area, the lady at the police station, now not quite so patient, managed to wind

274

down the conversation.

"Mrs. Brøttum again," sighed the uniformed officer to her colleague at the central switchboard in Lillehammer police station as she threw the note into the wastepaper basket.

Not very far from the station, two other uniformed policemen were enjoying a late dinner break. Three hot dogs and a large order of fries each. They were sitting on a hard, rigidly mounted concrete bench, scowling across at a pretty, neat woman in old-fashioned clothes who sat at the far end, beside the fairly busy highway. She was eating the same as them, but not as much. And not as fast.

"I'll bet that woman over there's not Norwegian," one of the officers said, his mouth full of food. "Look at those clothes!"

"Her hair's too light," the other one said, wiping his mouth with the back of his hand. "Her hair's far too light."

"She might be Turkish," the first one insisted. "Or Yugoslavian. They're sometimes blonde, you know!"

"Her over there's not a foreigner."

The other man did not give up. Neither did the first.

"Let's bet on it," he challenged. "I'll wager three hot dogs and one order of fries."

Thinking about it, the other man peered over at the small figure. She had now obviously realized they were interested in her, as she stood up abruptly and stepped quickly over to the trash can with what was left of her food.

"Okay."

The other took him on. They both got to their feet and approached the lady, who looked panic-stricken.

"I think you're damn right, Ulf," the doubter said. "She's scared of us in any case."

"Hello there," the first one shouted, confident of victory. "Stop a minute!"

The woman with the bizarre clothing stopped suddenly. She looked over at them, terrified.

"You're not from these parts, are you?"

He was friendly enough in a way.

"No, I not from here."

"Where are you from, then?"

"I from Iran, asylum seeker."

"Oh, yes. Well, have you got any papers on you?"

"No papers here, but where I live."

"And where's that, then?"

Of course she had forgotten what it was called. Moreover, she would hardly have been able to pronounce Gudbrandsdalen

Guesthouse if she had all the time in the world. Instead she simply pointed uncertainly up the road.

"Up there."

"Up there, yes, well," one of the policemen repeated, glancing at his colleague. "I think you'd better come with us. We'll have to check this out more closely."

They did not notice that the woman had tears in her eyes, or that she was trembling. They did not pay very much attention at all.

When the little Iranian woman did not appear for supper at the Gudbrandsdalen Guesthouse, Mrs. Brøttum came to the conclusion that her tip-off had been followed up. Humming cheerfully, she splashed out on an extra slice of cucumber for the buttered slices of bread with liver paste. She was exceedingly pleased.

In a cell at Lillehammer police station, the Iranian sat waiting for the police to check who she was. Unfortunately, she was brought in at the same time as the change of shift. The two who had placed a bet on her nationality were preoccupied with getting home to their wives and children, and asked their replacements to write the report. They promised on their honor to do so.

But of course they forgot. And so the

woman sat there, without anyone actually knowing where she was.

WEDNESDAY, JUNE 9

It was raining cats and dogs. Not to mention elephants and minke whales. It was as though everything nature had held back for the past two months was pouring out all at once. The water splashed down onto the dry earth that was totally unable to absorb such enormous amounts at the one time. Which led to the rain instead taking a shortcut to the sea by turning the streets into riverbeds. Åkebergveien looked as though the River Aker was in spring flood. It cascaded and streamed, and three traffic policemen were standing in rubber boots and rain attire, wondering when the water would reach the level when it would quite simply sweep the parked cars away. There was traffic chaos in Oslo.

Even the farmers, who, during the long period of drought, with their usual pessimism, had predicted the worst crops in living memory, as they did every single year, whether there was too much rain, too little rain, too little sun or too much, were of the opinion that there had to be limits. Now the harvest was certainly in peril. This was a total natural disaster.

Only the young folks were delighted. After the long heat wave, even a sudden surprising storm could not change the fact that summer temperatures were here to stay. The mercury in the thermometers still pointed to eighteen degrees Celsius. The youngsters shrieked in glee as they frolicked in the downpour, wearing only their bathing trunks, despite their mothers' vociferous protests. It was to no avail. This was the most cheerful, most intense, warmest rainy weather anyone could ever remember.

The angels are mourning Kaldbakken, Hanne Wilhelmsen thought as she glanced out the window.

It was like sitting in a car inside a car wash. The rain was pounding so violently against the windowpanes that the outlines of everything outside were completely obliterated, creating a pale gray fog. She leaned her forehead against the cool glass, and a dewy rose formed beside her mouth.

The intercom instructed them all to come to the conference room. She looked at the clock. There would be a memorial ceremony at eight o'clock. She hated that kind of thing. But she went.

The superintendent appeared gloomier than usual, appropriately enough. He was wearing a suit for the occasion, still wet from his ankles to his knees. It looked rather sad and so was suitable from that point of view. Dampness clogged the air in the unventilated room. No one was dry, but everyone was warm. And most of them were genuinely sorry.

Kaldbakken could hardly be called a popular man. He was too reserved, too taciturn for that. Grumpy, some would say. He had, however, been decent in all his years there. Fair. It was more than could be said for several other bosses at the station. So when some individuals dried a tear during the superintendent's stammering memorial speech, it was not just for appearance's sake.

Hanne Wilhelmsen did not shed a tear, but she was sad. She and Kaldbakken had worked well together. They had rather different viewpoints about most things outside the large building in which they earned a living, but as a rule they were in agreement about everything to do with their investigations. Moreover, you're better off with the devil you know. Hanne had no idea who would be the chief inspector now. In the worst-case scenario, they would end up with someone from another section. But it would probably be a few days yet before anyone was appointed. The man should at least be allowed to go to his grave before his successor moved into his kippered office.

The superintendent was finished, and an awkward silence descended over the gathering. Chairs scraped, but no one made a move to leave. They were all uncertain whether the session was over, or whether the lengthy silence was part of the proceedings.

"Well, the show must go on," the superintendent said, coming to their rescue.

The room emptied in less than a minute.

Hanne Wilhelmsen had got it into her head she needed to find the Iranian woman from the ground floor. It was worrying that she had disappeared without a trace. In her own mind, she feared the lady was already lying somewhere with her throat cut, underneath a few feet of earth. The Saturday man could have altered his habits. At the very least, they ought to get hold of her. It annoyed the detective inspector intensely that she had been carelessly superficial in her interview with her that first Monday. It hadn't seemed so important then. And of course she had so damn much to do.

Now it had at least been established that the woman in the secluded garden had been raped. Both one way and the other, in a manner of speaking. Hanne Wilhelmsen was sitting with the examination results from Forensics. They had not yet carried out any DNA analysis, that took a bloody long time, but semen had been identified in both the rectum and the vagina.

They had to find the lady from the ground floor. In the meantime, her home address was being covered. They had decided to do a fresh, thorough round of interviews with all the neighbors. Just to be on the safe side. Four police officers had allocated most of the day. She herself had more than enough to do in the office.

And outside the window, the prospect was still wet and gray.

Kristine Håverstad was unsure whether she would manage to kill someone who was sleeping. Although she felt a liberating sense of anticipation about what lay ahead, she wished she had a more effective weapon than a knife. A gun would be the best thing. Then she could taunt him. Take the upper hand, place him in the same situation he had forced her into. That would be best of all. That would be the fairest thing. Then he could pray to God not to die. She would take her time. Perhaps compel him to take off his clothes, to stand before her totally defenseless and stark naked, while she had both clothes and a gun.

Her father had a gun in his bedroom. She knew that, but she didn't know the first thing about guns. What she did know, however, was the most effective and deadly place to stab a knife into someone. But she needed some time. He had to be sleeping heavily. Between three and five o'clock people sleep most deeply. Between three and five she would get him.

She would manage to kill him, even though he was sleeping. But it was far from being the way she would have preferred.

The woman from Iran was sitting in a detention cell in Lillehammer for the fourteenth hour. She had been fed, as everyone detained there was. She had received nothing else. She did not challenge it and did not utter a word. That's the way it should be.

Last night she had not slept at all. There were so many noises and far too much light. What's more, she was terrified. She had sat in a cell twice before. It had not been as clean then. And she had not been given food either. But the uncertainty and anxiety had been exactly the same.

Creeping into a corner of the cell, she drew her knees up underneath her chin and sat without moving a muscle for several hours more.

"She's vanished without trace. No one has heard her, no one has seen her. Doesn't seem to have been home since Monday. Difficult to say, the neighbors tell me, because she kept herself to herself. Never a sound from that apartment, according to the two who live across from her."

Erik Henriksen looked like a drowned red fox. A little puddle had already formed around him, becoming larger by the minute. Leaning forward, he shook his head vigorously.

"Hey, there's no need to make me as wet as you!" Hanne Wilhelmsen protested.

"You should see that weather," Erik said excitedly. "It's unbelievable! It's pouring, it's bucketing, up to here in lots of places!"

He made a light karate chop on his own knee and beamed.

"It's almost impossible to drive a car! The motor gets drowned!"

He did not need to tell her. Hanne Wilhelmsen thought it looked as though the water would soon reach her window on the second floor. The traffic policemen in Åkebergveien had given up an hour earlier, and now the road was completely closed. In fact, people in the police station had gone from cracking lively jokes about the burst of rain to appearing legitimately concerned. The traffic chaos was no longer only a source of irritation. An ambulance had broken down when the engine became too wet in a small lake in Thorvald Meyers gate. They were so near Accident and Emergency that no harm was done; the patient had simply got soaked when the paramedics had to lift the stretcher between them, wading the two hundred meters or so down to the emergency room, as they carried the old lady with the broken femur. But worse things could happen. No one was particularly afraid of fire at the moment, but it was frightening to contemplate that the city's infrastructure was in the process of breaking down entirely. Two telecommunications areas had collapsed after a base station was flooded. A generator was close to stalling at Ullevål Hospital.

"What are the meteorologists saying?"

"No idea," Erik said, leaning against the window and looking outside. "But I say it won't let up for quite a while."

The superintendent entered as Erik left. He had removed his jacket but was still uncomfortably dressed in his suit trousers, which had clearly been purchased several kilos earlier. He pinched the trouser legs at the thigh before sitting down.

"We won't manage it before Saturday, will we?"

It was actually more a statement of fact than a question. Hanne therefore found no reason to reply.

"What are we doing now?" he asked, this time looking for an answer.

"I've sent four men out to Kristine Håverstad's apartment building. They're going to interview all the neighbors again. More thoroughly this time."

She stared slightly uneasily at the wet patch where Erik had stood.

"It's embarrassing. I should have been more meticulous the first time."

That was true. The superintendent, however, certainly knew why she had not been. He rubbed his face and sniffed.

"Damn it, with this change in the weather we'll all come down with colds. That's all we need now. An influenza epidemic."

Sighing deeply and sniffing again, he realized that Hanne Wilhelmsen still appeared concerned about her rather deplorable contribution to the rape case of the previous week. When they still had time. Perhaps enough time to prevent last Saturday's bloodbath.

"Well, Hanne," he said kindly, pushing his chair closer to her. "It was a rape. A horrible but unfortunately otherwise fairly ordinary rape. What should you have done? With all the rest we have to do? If you are right in this theory of yours that it's the same person behind the Saturday night massacres as well as this rape — and I think you are — then that's something we know now. We didn't know it a week ago."

Halting, he drew a rough and noisy breath, and sneezed violently.

"Do you know how many we'd need to be here in this section if we were to investigate every single rape to the degree it deserves?"

Hanne shook her head.

"Me neither."

He sneezed again.

"That's life. We have too few staff. Rape is a difficult crime. We can't spend much time on such things. Sorry to say."

His apology was heartfelt, and Hanne knew that. But the superintendent would not have had the job he had if it weren't for his extremely flexible and pragmatic character. Rape was a difficult crime to prove. The police needed to prove things. That was the way it was.

"Have you done anything other than talk to the neighbors?"

"Well, I'm waiting for the Forensics results. Not that whatever they come up with will be of any real use. But it would be good to have the proof ready if we find a culprit. Stumble over one."

A weary smile accompanied the final sentence.

"What's more, we're still pursuing the Iranian woman. I'm not happy about her disappearing act. I can't see any reason for her going missing. Either she's afraid of something, and then I would really like to know what she's scared of. Or who. Or perhaps she's joined her Asian sisters and is lying somewhere in the mud."

The superintendent knocked on wood, on the desk.

"Well, if she's still in the country and isn't dead . . ."

To be on the safe side, he knocked on the desktop one more time.

". . . then she'll turn up. Sooner or later."

"Let's sincerely hope it'll be sooner," Hanne Wilhelmsen said. "By the way, d'you know anything about this weather? It's beginning to be slightly sinister, you know!"

"It'll probably let up in the course of the evening. But it's going to continue to rain fairly heavily, or so the meteorologists say. But God only knows."

He stood up with difficulty. "Keep me posted. I'll be here all afternoon."

"Me too," Hanne Wilhelmsen responded.

"Besides . . ."

He turned abruptly in the doorway.

"The funeral's on Monday. Are you going to be there?"

"Yes, if the world's still spinning on Monday, yes I will."

It goes without saying that the weather was a disappointment. They had planned to start at the bustling center of Aker Brygge and from there go barhopping. It was not really possible. In fact, there were good grounds to doubt whether Aker Brygge was even still in existence.

"Crazy cool weather," Terje said enthusiastically. "Let's go swimming!"

The suggestion did not even receive a response. However, although the weather had put a stop to their original plans, a gang of students in the prime of life would not let the opportunity of a real party slip by.

"I've a proposal," Kristine said, who, as far as the others could make out, still looked rather poorly after her bout of influenza. "I've got plenty to drink at home. I'm staying at my dad's at the minute." She swiftly backtracked.

"I was so unwell. Better staying there. What about going to your place, Cathrine, and I'll get some wine and raid the fridge. Maybe we can have a late-night party. Dad will be sure to say it's okay."

It was a brilliant idea. Two more hours of study and then they would meet up at Cathrine's.

It was seven o'clock, and the rain had moderated somewhat. The window in Hanne Wilhelmsen's office was no longer a gray, blurred surface. Outside, she could now discern the roof of the garage where the patrol cars were housed as well as the used-car showroom on the other side of the street. The rain was making the picture just a little unclear. But it would be a downright lie to say the weather was fine.

One by one the constables had returned, drenched to the skin, after questioning the neighbors. Bringing up the rear was the trainee, who had actually thought it was all quite exciting. Now they were all sitting in their respective offices, writing their reports.

"Not a single one of you is going before

everybody's finished," she declared emphatically when they grumbled about the unpaid overtime.

"Bloody slave driver," one of them took the liberty of saying when she was out of earshot. "Is she going to be the new chief inspector, then?"

They wrote and wrote. Two of them had ventured in with finished products and hopeful smiles, only to be rejected peremptorily and sent back. Finally a bundle of twenty-four A4 sheets was sitting on Hanne Wilhelmsen's desk. Now dismissed, they rushed off like schoolboys on the last day before the summer vacation.

They still had no clue about the Iranian woman's disappearance. It was seriously starting to worry her deeply. But now it was past nine o'clock, and she was dead tired. She ought to read these reports conscientiously before she left. There might be something in them.

"Hardly," she said to herself after some thought.

However, she took the reports with her, for safety's sake. She could read them at home. Before she went, she made sure the central switchboard knew to phone her as soon as they heard anything about the Iranian. Or more correctly, if they heard anything about her.

The weather seemed to add extra spice to the party. The rain was battering the windowpane like a real autumn evening, and inside was warm and dry with plenty to drink. Two of the boys were now trying to fry deep-frozen fillet steaks.

"I'll have mine raw," Torill shouted.

"Raw," mumbled the boy who was frying. "She'll be lucky if it's any less than frozen solid."

Finn Håverstad had shown neither pleasure nor concern when Kristine arrived home and unexpectedly declared she was going to a party. She didn't look in a particularly festive mood. But he had given his blessing for taking one of the cases of wine. They had hardly exchanged a glance. When she was out the door, and the young man she had come with had bowed and scraped his way behind her, he had felt a kind of relief that she was out of the house. If he were fortunate, she would be away all night. It looked like it, if the amount of wine they had taken was anything to go by.

He had other things to do. Other things to think about.

Kristine sat drinking next to nothing. It was extremely difficult, as Terje was watching her like a hawk. As soon as she had taken a couple of sips, he was standing there ready to refill her glass. In the end, she moved away, to sit beside a huge yucca plant. Of course Terje moved as well. It didn't matter. On the contrary, in fact.

The party went as student parties usually do. They drank and yelled, and tucked into the fillet steak that was charred on the outside and frozen on the inside. They ate baked potatoes and made claret punch as the night drew on. They were dreading their examinations and looking forward to the summer. They made short-term plans about InterRail trips and long-term plans about doctorates and brain surgery.

When the church clock, outlined indistinctly on the other side of the road, struck twelve hollow notes, they were all extremely drunk. Except Kristine Håverstad. She had performed the feat of sitting there all evening without drinking more than a single glass. The leaves of the yucca plant, on the other hand, were already starting to droop.

It was now almost exactly sixteen hours since the Iranian woman had been taken into custody by two policemen in Lillehammer following a wager. Still no one had spoken to her. Still she had not uttered a peep of protest about her treatment. Still she sat, frightened to death and desperately tired, in the far corner of a detention cell with her knees tucked underneath her chin. The food sat untouched on a tray at the other end of the room. She was certain she was going to die. And so she closed her eyes and thanked Allah for every minute that passed without anyone coming to fetch her.

The shift supervisor that night was an industrious chap from Gausdal. He was thirty-two years old and had a glowing future in the police and prosecution services. He was studying law part-time and managed to follow the normal rate of progression in his studies despite working full-time and having a wife and two children and a newly built detached house. A man like him did not sleep on the job.

But it was tempting. He yawned. The crazy weather had caused the police service a pile of work that wasn't normally their province. But when everyone else lets them down, people call the police. He had directed his troops through everything from flooded basements to people trapped in their cars with water up to the door handles. Now the rain had eased for a few hours, and the town seemed to have fallen silent at last. But he should not doze off.

His uniform was beginning to be a bit tight. His wife called it his extra comfort layer. She might be right. He was damn well-off. Good job, beautiful family, secure financial position, and pleasant in-laws. A boy from Gausdal could hardly ask for more. Smiling, he went on a round of the cells.

"You're here again, Reidar," he greeted an old regular with no teeth whose blood alcohol count was 4. The prisoner stood up unsteadily, swaying with pleasure at seeing him again.

"But is it you, Frogner, is it really you?" Then he fell over.

Frogner laughed. "I think you should lie down again, Reidar. It'll be better in the morning, you'll see."

He knew almost all of them. Not all of them could be awakened. In that case, he went inside and shook them, forcing one eye open to check they were still alive. They were indeed. When he reached the farthest cell, he was astonished.

A woman was sitting curled up in the far corner. She was not sleeping anyway, although her eyes were closed. They were squeezed tightly together, and even from the bars on the door he could see that her eyelids were trembling.

Slowly withdrawing the bolt, he opened the heavy metal door. The woman did not visibly react, just pinched her eyes closed even more tightly.

Knut Frogner had grown up on a farm. He had seen frightened animals before. What's more, he had two children and good common sense. He remained standing at the door.

"Hello," he said softly.

Still no reaction.

He crouched down to make himself smaller.

"There's no danger."

She opened her eyes gingerly. They were dark blue.

"Who are you?"

Perhaps she did not speak Norwegian. There was something foreign about her, despite her eyes.

"Who are you?" he repeated in his schoolboy English from Gausdal.

It was not easy. The woman did not answer at all, and now she had closed her eyes again. He approached her with short, slow steps and sat down again on his haunches. He placed a hand on her knee, and she froze. But at least she opened her eyes.

"Who are you?" he repeated.

The bundle he had read contained no report about any foreigner being brought in. In fact, there was no report about any woman brought in at all. A deeply uneasy feeling began to grip the policeman. How long had this lady actually been sitting here?

He understood one thing at least. It was no use trying to talk to her in here. Carefully, but firmly, he raised the woman into a standing position. She had obviously been sitting in the same posture for a long time, as a painful expression crossed her face when, with stiff movements, she allowed herself to stand on her own two feet. She did not smell of alcohol. She could not have been arrested for being drunk and disorderly. But to judge by her clothes, she was from Farawaystan.

Taking her by the hand, he led her out of the cell. When they reached the common room, he sent the three exhausted officers packing and switched off the video they had been watching. Then he installed the woman on the uncomfortable settee.

"I really need to know what your name is," he said, trying to appear as pleasant as it was possible to be while wearing a uniform.

She mumbled a name. Her voice was weak, and he had no chance of understanding what she said.

"What?" he said quickly, shaking his head and cupping his hand behind his ear. That ought to be international enough.

She repeated her name, more clearly this time. It did not help at all, as he could not make head or tail of it.

Feverishly he looked around for something to write on. There was a piece of greaseproof paper at the end of the table, with a leftover brown cheese sandwich on top. He grabbed the paper, paying no attention to the scrap of bread falling on the floor. Then he patted his breast pocket and located a pen. He placed both of these in front of her. Slowly and apprehensively she lifted the pen and wrote her name, at least something that might resemble a name, on the paper.

"Do you speak Norwegian at all?"

Now she dared to nod her head.

"How long have you been here?"

"Don't know."

These were the first words she had spoken in almost thirty-six hours. The policeman swore under his breath and then moved heaven and earth to find out who this woman actually was.

Finn Håverstad did not have much to do.

The extreme weather had seemed at first

to be an unexpected hindrance. Now it looked like a blessing. Everybody was staying indoors. The rapist as well. Håverstad had arrived at eleven o'clock and could see both movement and light in the terraced house in Bærum. When he discovered that, he felt a mixture of heartfelt relief and disconcerting anxiety. Deep inside, he had cherished a hope that the man would be away, had left or perhaps had visitors. Overnight guests. Then he would have been forced to postpone his actions. For a while.

But strongest of all was the relief.

The rain was still falling steadily, though it was not as much of a deluge as earlier. It was tempting to remain sitting in the car. However, he was afraid of being seen. Moreover, the last few days had shown him it was not so smart to leave your own car parked beside a crime scene. True enough, he was not planning to get away with his crime, but he would prefer to have some time. Time to calm down afterward. Several hours, a day or two. Perhaps as much as a week. He did not know yet, but he wanted to have the opportunity to decide for himself.

He therefore contented himself with stopping for a few minutes with the motor running, enough to be sure the rapist was at home. Then he let the car jolt across two speed bumps and around a corner. A row of terraced apartments, four stories high and one hundred meters in length, was situated on the left-hand side. The wives' cars, for which there was insufficient room in the underground parking facility, were sitting in an enormous parking lot. He left his BMW there, between an old Honda and a smart new Opel Corsa. It looked as though it enjoyed the company.

The Glock was ready for use. He had stuffed it into the waistband of his trousers, more for lack of a better place than because it was practical. It felt uncomfortable but was at least dry.

He walked the couple of hundred meters back. At the end of the road leading to the culprit's house, he came to a halt. Across from the terrace of houses he could discern some kind of yard, with various items of play equipment and a few benches. They hadn't been visible from the other side, since the row comprised ten connected houses, shielding it from view. From the gable wall across to the yard there were approximately twenty to thirty meters before an outcrop rose fairly steeply, probably making the play yard unpleasantly dark, even on better days than this. Momentarily,

Finn Håverstad wondered whether he should alter his plans and attempt instead to enter from that side. It was far more sheltered, both with respect to the road and the detached houses situated farther down. On the other hand, a stranger on the road would probably arouse less attention. If any at all.

He would keep to his original plan. He turned up his raincoat hood and tried to walk at as normal a pace as possible over to the fifth house in the terrace. He remained standing there for a split second. It was now half past midnight, with nobody in sight. Most of the windows were in darkness. He crept into a shrubbery where three hedges met, only eight meters from the rapist's residence.

Finn Håverstad sat there waiting.

Terje had not needed to be asked twice. He would probably have suggested it himself, had he not been invited. Overjoyed and extremely drunk, he stumbled out to the taxi Kristine had at last been able to get hold of, after waiting forty minutes in an annoying telephone queue. He was being allowed to go home with her. In the middle of the night. Which could of course mean only one thing, and anticipation kept him awake nearly all the way home. But only nearly. When they swung into the courtyard in front of Kristine Håverstad's childhood home in Volvat, she had a hard struggle to force the boy awake. Eventually she had to request help from the taxi driver to get him as far as the entrance. The taxi driver had been grouchy as hell about having to leave his vehicle in the soaking wet weather, especially as the courtyard was one enormous puddle. Muttering curses, he had dropped the boy onto the hallway floor.

"You'll not have much fun with him there tonight," he said sullenly, becoming slightly more cheerful when Kristine paid him fifty kroner more than the rate on the taximeter.

"But good luck anyway," he mumbled then, with a hint of a smile.

It had not been the intention to get him so sloshed. It took her almost five minutes to haul, drag, and carry the boy the eight meters or so into the bedroom. The difficulty was even greater of course because she wanted to avoid waking her father.

The bed was narrow, but she had brought boys there before. Terje was fighting his own determined battle to awaken for what might be the big moment of his life. But when Kristine had taken off all his clothes and laid him down comfortably in a lovely bed, all hope was lost. He snored. It didn't seem to bother him in the least when she pulled the quilt off him and turned him around, so his neat, hairy backside was presented conveniently for a jab. She had prepared the injection earlier and it lay just below the bed. Since he was more blotto than she had reckoned, strictly speaking, she released a few milliliters with the plunger. Ninety would do. Ninety milliliters of Nozinan. At the Blue Cross center, they used up to three hundred to give the most cantankerous drunkards some well-deserved hours of sleep each time they went on a drinking spree for days, barely remembering their own names. But Terje was far from being an alcoholic, although currently he must have well over two per mille of ethanol in his veins. Moreover, he was so far gone she fleetingly doubted whether it was at all necessary to ensure he would sleep through the entire night. The doubt did not last long. She resolutely jabbed the syringe into the boy's left buttock, and there was no re-action. She injected the contents slowly into the muscle. When the plunger reached the base, she removed the needle carefully and pressed a ball of cotton wool firmly on the injection site for a few minutes. She then tidied up scrupulously. It had all been very

successful. When Terje regained consciousness late the next morning with her by his
side, he would have a thumping hangover,
but he would not be able to contradict her
when she thanked him for a wonderful
night. A boy in his prime, with more limited
experience than he would ever admit to,
would wonder a little, consider it deeply,
and then concoct an excellent, ego-
enhancing story about how marvelous it had
been.

Kristine Håverstad had arranged her
clumsy alibi. Her outer clothes were sod-
den, and she shivered as she put them back
on again. Her own car was sitting, affronted
and wet, at the far corner of the courtyard,
sufficiently distant from the house that she
would not wake anyone. As thanks for her
not bothering to put it in the garage the day
before, it refused to start.

She couldn't bloody start the car.

Hanne Wilhelmsen was trying to sleep. It
was difficult. Although the storm had diminished somewhat, the rain was lashing the
bedroom window, and the chimney was
howling with every violent gust of wind.
What's more, she had too much on her
mind.

The whole thing was hopeless. She was so

tired it was impossible to concentrate. The reports were lying half read on the table in the living room. At the same time, it was totally impossible to fall asleep. She changed position every other minute, in the hope of finding a heavenly posture, allowing her muscles to relax and her brain to stop spinning. Cecilie mumbled grumpily every time she tossed and turned.

Eventually she gave up. When all was said and done, it would be better if one of them managed to sleep. Carefully and almost soundlessly, she rose from the bed, unhooked the pink dressing gown from its hanger beside the door, and stepped into the living room. There, she collapsed into a chair and started on the reports once again.

The three officers had been relatively brief, in the concise language striving for precision that often became anything but and therefore irritated her enormously. The trainee on the other hand apparently had greater literary ambitions. He was in his element with metaphors and long sentences, writing here, there, and round about. Hanne smiled. The boy could actually write; even the spelling had only a couple of minor faults. But it was hardly very policeman-like.

Yes indeed. That boy had talent. He had

discovered that the family above the victim's residence had a neighbor directly opposite who sat quietly at the window, as though he were sleeping. The trainee, disappointed that nobody else had anything of value to contribute to the police investigation, had decided to go across the street. He had visited a weird eccentric who was obviously in the habit of watching everything going on in the little street. The man, whose age was impossible to estimate, had been quite hostile but also seemingly proud of his many archive files of this and that. Moreover, he was able to confirm that a man called Håverstad had been there a short time before.

Hanne Wilhelmsen was more awake now. Rolling her head vigorously a few times in an effort to bring more blood to her over-tired brain, she decided to make some coffee. She might as well give up on that particular night, as far as sleep and rest were concerned. She read the remainder of the page first. After that she no longer needed coffee, as she was wide awake.

Then the phone rang. Hanne's phone. She took three bounds to reach the hallway, hoping she could answer before it woke Cecilie.

"Wilhelmsen," she said softly, trying to drag the cable with her into the living room.

This caused the phone to clatter to the floor.

"Hello," she tried again, almost whispering.

"This is Villarsen. Central switchboard here. We've just received a report from Lillehammer. They've found the Iranian woman we were looking for."

"Get her here," Hanne Wilhelmsen said abruptly. "Immediately."

"They have a transport coming to Oslo early tomorrow. She'll be on that."

"No," Hanne Wilhelmsen replied. "She has to come here now. At once. Requisition something or other. A helicopter, if that's what it takes. Whatever. I'll be at the station in ten minutes."

"Do you really mean that about a helicopter?"

"I've hardly meant anything more seriously in all my life. Say hi to the prosecutor on duty and say it's a matter of life or death. Say hi to the commissioner, for that matter. I need to speak to that lady."

For once, something went smoothly in the huge, dilapidated building at Grønlandsleiret 44. Only twenty minutes after the conversation between the central switchboard and Detective Inspector Hanne Wilhelmsen, the female Iranian asylum seeker was sitting in a helicopter en route from Lillehammer to Oslo. Hanne had feared for a while that the weather would be an obstacle to air transport, but then she didn't know very much about helicopters. Now that the rain had subsided, there was probably not much of a problem. That it was stretching an already overstretched budget was something to argue about later.

The waiting time had to be put to good use. The Iranian was expected in three-quarters of an hour at the earliest. In the meantime, they had to try the oddball in the neighboring apartment building. The one with the car registration numbers. Seven car numbers from May 29, as he had shown the stripeless trainee rather unwillingly, though also with a touch of pride. Unfortunately, the inexperienced policeman had accepted the actual information about the number plates but had not made a note of them. Although it was now past one o'clock in the morning, Hanne Wilhelmsen felt it imperative to press E into making a useful contribution to society.

It turned out to be easier said than done. Now she was sitting in the central switchboard, the room in the middle of the police station. It was filled with the busy hum of quiet voices. Radio messages streamed in steadily from patrol cars on night duty in the capital city, from Fox and Bravo, Delta and Charlie, depending on who they were and what they were working on. They were given information and instructions in response, from uniformed policemen who now and again made an internal phone call to a sleepy prosecutor to clear an arrest or the forcing open of a door. Hanne Wilhelmsen was sitting on the second bench of the rows of seats along the sloping floor. She quickly found Kristine Håverstad's address on the enormous map of Oslo displayed on the wall directly opposite. She had been staring at it for several minutes. She was waiting nervously, full of grave misgivings, for a response from the patrol car that had been assigned the task. In the tension and distraction, she broke three pencils that most certainly hadn't committed any offense.

"Fox three-zero calling Zero-one."

"Zero-one to Fox three-zero. What happened?"

"He won't let us in."

"Won't let you in?"

"Either he isn't at home, or else he won't let us in. Probably the second, we think. Should we force the door?"

There had to be limits. Even though it was

extremely important to know what information Finn Håverstad had obtained from the simpleton, there was not a shred of justification for breaking in. She fleetingly considered dealing with all this shit afterward instead. But there wasn't a prosecuting attorney in the world who would give the go-ahead to such an obvious illegality.

"No." She sighed in forbearance. "Try a few more times all the same. Pester him. Keep your finger pressed on the doorbell. Zero-one out."

The car changed its mind. After tenaciously resisting Kristine Håverstad's enraged attempts to start the engine, it suddenly and inexplicably began to throb. It took barely half an hour to reach her destination.

She would not risk being seen. She had already decided two days earlier that it would have to take place between two and three o'clock. There was a while to go till then. In the meantime, it was important to remain hidden. It was possibly a mistake to leave home so early. On the other hand, she was now so close that in the worst-case scenario, if the car were to experience yet another insistent attack of retribution, she could use her legs. It would not take more than two or three minutes to jog over to the terraced house belonging to the man who had raped her.

The rain was doing her good. There were already small rivers running down her neck, on the inside of both her rain jacket and sweater. Normally this would have felt uncomfortable, but not now. She was cold but not shivering. She was numb but felt a new and unfamiliar peace surging through her body, a kind of complete and all-encompassing sense of control. Her thumping heartbeats were hard and regular but not too fast.

Facing her was a grove of trees, divided in two by a well-used broad path. In a clearing around the middle of the round little forest was a wooden bench, and she sat there. Above her, the sky was rumbling and furiously spitting bolts of lightning at the ground. The thunderclap was followed by a powerful crash as the entire grove was illuminated by a terrifying blue light. The rainy weather was a blessing, as it had chased all witnesses indoors. The thunderstorm, which now must be directly overhead, was worse. That kept people awake. But the weather was something no one could do anything about. It would have to be put to the test. She shook off the trace of unease that had restrained her following the

312

flash of lightning, again feeling levelheaded and prepared for what she had in mind.

The helicopter hovered like an intimidating, booming Thor only fifteen meters above the muddy patch of grass at the Jordal Amfi sports arena. It was oscillating heavily and steadily from side to side, like a pendulum attached to the lowering black cloud cover by an invisible cable. The monster was slowly closing in on the ground.

A uniformed policeman opened the door and jumped out before the helicopter had come completely to a standstill. He remained crouched over, waiting momentarily while the rotor blades continued to clatter threateningly above him. Then a small, slender figure in a red raincoat followed behind. She hesitated imperceptibly at the helicopter door but was whisked out rapidly by the impatient police officer. He took her hand and together they ran through the violent gusts of wind across the running track in the squelching mud.

Hanne Wilhelmsen was madly short of time but waited nevertheless for the helicopter pilot. He eventually arrived, pale and drawn.

"Should never have attempted this," he said, giving Hanne the idea that the journey had been far from enjoyable.

"We were struck by lightning," he muttered faintly from the passenger seat of the patrol car, parked with its motor running. The policeman and the Iranian witness were sitting silently in the backseat. They didn't need to say anything either. It took almost exactly ninety seconds until the police car swept into the backyard at Grønlandsleiret 44, where Hanne had arranged in advance for the gates to stand open to embrace them in welcome.

The pilot and the uniformed police officer looked after themselves. The asylum seeker accompanied Hanne to her office.

The detective inspector felt like a biathlete on her way to the shooting range. She had many questions but knew she had to create a sense of calm. On an impulse, she grasped the other woman's hand, leading her upstairs like a small child. Her hand was cold as ice and completely limp.

She has to talk. She simply has to talk.

Hanne Wilhelmsen was offering up a silent prayer. Finn Håverstad might of course be lying safely in his bed in Volvat. But he had obtained seven car registration numbers to exploit. That was two days ago. More than enough time for such a man. The Iranian simply must talk.

The woman remained standing stock-still, without making any move either to remove her rainwear or sit down. Hanne invited her to do both but received no response. She stepped across to her slowly, attempting to make contact.

Detective Inspector Hanne Wilhelmsen was twenty-five centimeters taller than the woman from Iran. Moreover, she was ten years older. Moreover, she was Norwegian. And moreover, she had a crazy amount to do. Without thinking that the gesture might be construed as humiliating, she therefore stretched out her hand and held the other woman's face. She held her underneath the chin, not unfriendly, not roughly, but quite firmly, and lifted the face to make eye contact.

"Listen," she said softly but with an intensity the woman could probably appreciate, despite her foreign language. "I know you're afraid of someone or other. He's been pestering you. God only knows what he's done. I can guarantee you one thing. He will be punished."

The woman did not even try to break free. She just stood there, with upturned face and a faraway look it was impossible to read anything into. Her arms were hanging listlessly by her sides, and the red raincoat was dripping relentlessly onto the floor.

"You must be dead tired. I am too."

She did not let go of the asylum seeker's face.

"I can assure you of one thing more. It makes no difference . . ."

Now she let go. As she rubbed herself across the eyes with the same hand, she felt an uncontrollable urge to weep. Not because she was sad, necessarily, but because she was exhausted and convinced she was too late. And because she was now going to say something she had never said before. Something that had been hanging over them all as an oppressive possibility since they had discovered the connection with the bloody FK numbers. Without anyone ever expressing the thought out loud.

"Even if the man is a policeman, you mustn't be afraid. I promise you, you have no reason to be scared."

It was the middle of the night, and Hanne Wilhelmsen was all she had. She was tired out and hungry. The fear had been sitting inside her so long it forced her to make a choice. It was as though she were waking up all of a sudden. She looked down at the wet raincoat and the puddle on the floor. She glanced fleetingly around the room, surprised, as though wondering where she was. Then she discarded her raincoat and sat gingerly on the edge of a chair.

"He said I had to sleep with him. Or I not allowed to stay in Norway."

"Who?" Hanne Wilhelmsen inquired quietly.

"It be very difficult, I know nobody . . ."

"Who?" the detective inspector repeated.

The phone rang. Hanne grabbed it furiously and barked a hello.

"Erik here."

There had not been a "no" in the constable's mouth since she had asked him to come in. One night with Hanne Wilhelmsen was one night with Hanne Wilhelmsen, regardless of the circumstances.

"Two things. We have the car numbers. The guy opened up eventually. What's more, there's no one at home in Finn Håverstad's house. At least there's no reply no matter how much you ring the bell."

That was what she expected. Finn Håverstad could of course have followed her advice and taken his daughter with him on vacation. But she knew very well that was not the case.

"Get the names of the car owners. Right away. Check them against . . ."

She halted suddenly, gazing at an enormous raindrop splashing at the top of the windowpane. When it had reached halfway down toward the sill, she continued.

"Check the names against people here at the station. Start with the Immigration Department."

Erik Henriksen didn't hesitate. He simply replaced the receiver. Hanne Wilhelmsen did the same. Then she wheeled around to face the witness, only to discover that the tiny woman was sobbing. Soundlessly and brokenheartedly. It was far beyond Hanne Wilhelmsen's powers to comfort her. Of course she could tell her how lucky she actually was, since she hadn't been at home on May 29. Of course she could inform her that if she had been, she would very probably now be lying somewhere or other in the Oslo area, several feet under, with her throat cut. Not much comfort.

Hanne brushed it aside and said instead, "I'll promise you several things tonight. I swear you'll be allowed to remain here. I'll make sure of that whether or not you choose to tell me now who the man is. But it would help me enormously . . ."

"He called Frydenberg. I not know the other name."

Hanne Wilhelmsen stormed out the door.

It was about time to make a start. She felt

lighthearted and invigorated, almost happy. The lights at the window of the fifth house in the terrace had been switched off over an hour ago. The thunderstorm had moved off in an eastwardly direction and would most likely reach Sweden before dawn.

At the entrance door, he remained standing, listening, unnecessarily but to be on the safe side. Then he pulled a crowbar from one of the pockets in his voluminous raincoat. It was wet, but the rubber handle made the grip good and firm. It took only a few seconds to break the door open. Surprisingly simple, he thought, placing his hand tentatively on the doorplate, which gave way.

He entered the apartment.

Her eyes skimmed the sheet he showed her. There.

Olaf Frydenberg. Owner of an Opel Astra, with a registration number that was observed by an odd little chap in the short street where Kristine Håverstad was raped. A police sergeant based at Oslo police station's Immigration Department. He had been working there for four months. Earlier, he had been in post at Asker and Bærum police station. Residence: Bærum.

"Shit," Hanne Wilhelmsen said. "Shit,

shit. Bærum."

She stared at Erik Henriksen wildly for a
second.

"Phone Asker and Bærum. Send them to
the address. Say they need to be armed. Say
we're on our way as well. And ask for approval, for God's sake."

There was always trouble when police
trespassed onto one another's patch. But
wild horses couldn't keep Hanne Wilhelmsen away from this particular patch.

Down at the crime desk stood a bewildered prosecutor; on top of everything else,
this was his first shift in the post. Fortunately, he was quietly and unsuspectingly
manipulated by a sensible supervisor with a
police college background and twenty years'
experience. Hanne was granted her patrol
car and a uniformed police inspector for
company. The supervisor assured her sotto
voce that he would arrange permission to
deploy weapons by the time they reached
their destination.

"Sirens?"

It was Police Inspector Audun Salomonsen who was wondering. He had, without
asking her, sat in the driver's seat. Hanne
was quite happy with that.

"Yes," she replied without further thought.
"At least for the moment."

■ ■ ■ ■

The bedroom was located where bedrooms usually are. Not on the same level as the living room. The hallway was on the same floor as two bedrooms, a bathroom, and something resembling a storeroom. A pine staircase led up to the first floor, where he knew he would find a living room and kitchen.

For one reason or another, he removed his shoes. A considerate kind of gesture, far too considerate, he thought as he pondered whether he should put his muddy boots on again. But they were squelching. He would leave them where they were.

He had problems closing the front door properly. When he forced entry, he had broken the frame so the doorjamb no longer fitted. Carefully and as soundlessly as possible, he wedged the door as far closed as it permitted. He was uncertain how long it would hold in this wind.

Both bedroom doors were shut. It was undeniably of some importance that he chose correctly. The man might be a light sleeper.

Finn Håverstad reasoned which of the rooms had to be larger, from the way the doors were situated and his observations of the house from outside. He chose correctly.

A big double bed was made on one side only. The quilt was neatly folded three times, crosswise, like an enormous pillow. On the other side, near the door, lay a figure. It was not possible to see the person, who had pulled the quilt so far up that only a few tufts of hair were poking out at the headboard. They were blond. Closing the door quietly behind him, Finn Håverstad fished out the service pistol from his waistband, performed the loading motions, and crossed the room to the sleeping man.

With exaggeratedly slow movements, like a slow-motion film, he moved the mouth of the gun toward the head in the bed. Then he pushed it suddenly and firmly against something that had to be the forehead. It had the required effect. The man woke and tried to sit up.

"Lie still," Håverstad snapped.

Whether it was the command or the fact the guy had now caught sight of the gun that caused him to lie down again was not certain. At any rate, he was now wide awake.

"What the fuck's this?" he said, trying to appear pissed off.

It did not work. His face was flushed with fear. His eyes were blinking and nostrils flaring in rhythm with his heavy, intense breathing.

"Lie completely still and listen to me first," Håverstad said in a voice so calm it surprised him. "I won't harm you. At least not seriously. We're just going to have a chat. But I swear one thing on my daughter's life — if you as much as raise your voice, I'll shoot you."

The man in the bed stared at the gun. Then he looked at his attacker. There was something familiar about the face, but at the same time he was one hundred percent sure he had never seen this guy before. Something about the eyes.

"What the fuck do you want?" he ventured again.

"I want to talk to you. Stand up. Raise your hands in the air. Don't drop them."

The man again tried to get up. It was difficult. The bed was low and he was told not to use his hands. Finally he was on his feet.

Finn Håverstad was ten centimeters taller than his victim. It gave him the advantage he needed now that the rapist was on his feet and appeared far less vulnerable than when lying in the bed. He was wearing pajamas, some kind of cotton material, without a fly or buttons. The top was a sweater with a V-neck. It looked something like a tracksuit. It was washed-out and rather tight, and the dentist took a step back when he saw the muscular body bulging beneath the flimsy material.

The tiny recognition of uncertainty was all that was required. The rapist threw himself at Håverstad, and they both crashed against the wall only a meter behind. It proved helpful. Håverstad got the support he needed, with his back firmly against the wall, while the other man lost his balance and fell onto one knee. Quick as a flash he attempted to regain his footing, but he was too late. The butt of the gun hit him above the ear, and he fell to the floor. The pain was intense, but he did not lose consciousness. Håverstad used the opportunity to wrestle the kneeling man backward toward the bed, where he remained sitting with his back to the thick feather mattress, rubbing his head and feeling sorry for himself. Håverstad stepped across his legs, pointing the gun at him the entire time. He grabbed the pillow beside the headboard, and before the kneeling man had time to think, his attacker had forced his arm against the mattress and placed the pillow over it. He then buried the gun deep inside the downy mass and pulled the trigger.

The gunshot sounded like a faint plop.

They were both taken aback, Håverstad by what he had done and also that the shot was so faint, the other that the pain was delayed. Then it struck him. He was about to scream, when the sight of the barrel waving in his face made him clench his teeth. He pulled his arm toward his chest and moaned. It was pouring with blood.

"Now perhaps you understand what I mean," Håverstad whispered.

"I'm a policeman," the other groaned.

A policeman? Was that contemptible, inhuman destructive machine a policeman? Håverstad wondered for a moment what he should do with this information. Then he shrugged it off. It made no difference. Nothing made any difference. He felt stronger than ever.

"Get up," he ordered once more, and this time the policeman didn't attempt to do anything at all. Continuing to moan faintly, he allowed himself to be ordered upstairs to the first floor. Håverstad was careful to follow several paces behind, fearing that the other man would fling himself backward.

The living room was in darkness with curtains closed. Only a glimmer from the kitchen, where the light above the stove was switched on, made it possible to see anything at all. Letting the policeman stand beside the stairs, Håverstad turned on a light on the wall at the kitchen entrance. He remained standing, surveying the room. He waved the other man over to a wicker chair. The policeman thought at first he was to sit down, but was forestalled.

"Position yourself with your back to the back of the chair!"

The policeman had difficulty remaining upright. Blood still streaming from his arm, he blanched, and even in the faint light Håverstad could see the terror in his face and the sweat on his high forehead. It did him an unspeakable amount of good.

"I'm bleeding to death," the policeman complained.

"You're not bleeding to death."

It was quite difficult to tie the man's arms and legs tightly with only one hand. Occasionally he was forced to use both hands, but all the same he did not release his grip on the pistol and kept it pointed at the other man. Fortunately, he had foreseen the problem and brought with him four lengths of rope, already cut. Finally, the policeman was tied up. His legs were spread and each was tied to a chair leg. His arms were bent backward and attached to the part of the armrest where it curved upward to form the chair back. The chair was not particularly heavy, and the man was having problems retaining his balance. The way he was standing, he seemed continually to be about to fall over. Lifting a huge television from a little glass cabinet with wheels, Håverstad ripped out the cables and dropped the set onto the seat of the wicker chair.

He stepped into the kitchen and opened a cupboard. Wrong cupboard. At the third attempt, he found what he was searching for: a large, ordinary carving knife, made in Finland. He ran his thumb along the edge and returned to the living room.

The man was almost prostrate and looked like a dead jumping jack. The ropes prevented him from collapsing altogether, and he was sitting in an absurd, almost comical position: straddled, with knees bent and arms helplessly twisted backward. Finn Håverstad dragged a chair in front of him and sat down.

"Do you remember what you were doing on May twenty-ninth?"

The man obviously had no idea.

"In the evening? Saturday a week and a half ago?"

Now the policeman knew what had seemed familiar about this guy. The eyes. The chick in Homansbyen.

Until now he had been afraid. He was

afraid about the injury to his arm, and he was afraid of this grotesque character who was apparently deriving perverse pleasure from tormenting him. But he hadn't thought he was going to die. Until now.

"Take it easy," Håverstad said. "I'm still not going to kill you. We're just going to talk for a while."

Then he stood up and took hold of the other man's pajama top. He pushed the knife inside it and pulled it down so the sweater was suddenly converted into a jacket. A tattered, lopsided jacket. He took hold of the waistband of his trousers and repeated the process. The trousers fell down, stopping at thigh level because of his sprawled legs. But everything significant was exposed, naked and defenseless.

Finn Håverstad sat down on the chair again.

"Now we're going to talk," he said, with an Austrian pistol in one hand and a large Finnish carving knife in the other.

Although she had originally intended to wait for another half hour, she got to her feet and headed for her destination. Waiting was a nightmare.

In fact it took less time than she had thought. After only a minute at a brisk pace, she had reached the street leading past the rapist's abode. It was totally deserted. Slowing down, she gave herself a shake and moved off in the direction of the house.

"Turn off the sirens."

They were well outside their own district. Police Inspector Salomonsen was a competent driver. Even now, on side roads and with intersections every twenty meters or so, he was driving rapidly and smoothly, without too much skidding or discomfort. She had briefed him on the situation, and via the radio they had received the go-ahead for use of weapons.

She watched the illuminated numbers on the dashboard. It would soon be two o'clock.

"Don't slow down," Hanne Wilhelmsen said.

"Do you really have any idea what you've done?"

The policeman sitting tightly bound in his own living room had a vague idea. He had made a major mistake. It should never have happened. He had miscalculated. Hugely. Now he could only comfort himself with the fact that no one had ever taken revenge in such a way before.

Not in Norway, he said to himself. Not in Norway.

"You have defiled my daughter," the man snarled, leaning forward in his seat. "You have destroyed and despoiled my little girl!"

The tip of the knife grazed the rapist's genitals, and he groaned in alarm.

"Now you're afraid," the other man whispered, letting the knife roam playfully over his groin. "Now perhaps you are just as scared as my daughter was. But you didn't care about that."

By then the rapist could not tolerate any more. Taking a deep breath, he emitted a deranged, piercing howl that could have wakened the dead.

Plunging forward, Finn Håverstad drove the huge knife from behind, upward in an enormous arc, gathering speed and strength. The point struck the rapist in his sprawling crotch, penetrating his testicles, perforating the musculature in his groin, and disappearing into his abdominal cavity, where it stuck fast, the blade having ruptured an artery.

The scream stopped as suddenly as it had started. The sound was chopped straight off, and it became eerily silent. The rapist collapsed completely, the chair threatening to topple over, despite the weight of the television set on the seat.

Someone came storming up the stairs. Finn Håverstad turned around quietly as he heard the footsteps, wondering only how the neighbors had been alerted so quickly. Then he saw who it was.

Neither of them uttered a word. Kristine Håverstad rushed toward him, in what he anticipated would be an embrace. Stretching his arms out to his daughter, he was knocked sideways when she instead clawed along his arm to grab hold of the pistol. It dropped to the floor and she retrieved it before he managed to regain his footing.

He was much larger than her and far stronger. All the same, he was not able to prevent a shot being fired as he gripped her arm, firmly but not too hard, since he wanted to avoid hurting her. The bang made them both jump skyward. Terror stricken, she let go of the gun, and he let go of her. For several seconds they stood staring at each other, before Kristine grabbed hold of the knife handle protruding from the rapist's loins, like a bizarre rock-hard spare penis. When she withdrew the knife, the blood gushed out.

Hanne Wilhelmsen and Audun Salomonsen were taken aback that their colleagues from Asker and Bærum had not yet arrived on the scene. The silent road lay in darkness, with no sign of the anticipated flashing blue lights. The car juddered to a halt in front of the terrace of houses. As they ran toward the entrance, they heard the sound of police sirens not too far off in the distance.

The door had been forced. It was wide open. They had arrived too late.

When Detective Inspector Hanne Wilhelmsen reached the top of the stairs, she was confronted by a sight she knew would stay with her forever.

Tied to a chair with his arms twisted behind him, his legs sprawled at an angle, and his chin resting on his chest, hung her colleague Olaf Frydenberg. He resembled a frog. He was almost naked, and a river of blood was streaming down from his pubic region to a rapidly growing puddle at his feet. Before carrying out any examination, she knew he was dead.

Nevertheless, she held her gun in front of her with both hands, pointing away to a corner of the living room and ordering the two people there to stand back from the victim. They obeyed immediately, with eyes downcast, like dutiful children.

There was no pulse. She forced an eyelid open. The eyeball stared dead and senseless at her. She speedily started to loosen the ropes around his wrists and ankles.

"We'll try artificial respiration," she said obstinately to her colleague. "Get the first aid equipment."

"I did it," Finn Håverstad interrupted suddenly from his corner of the room.

"It was me!"

Kristine Håverstad sounded desperate.

"He's lying! It was me!"

Wheeling around abruptly, Hanne Wilhelmsen scrutinized the two of them more closely. She felt no anger. Not even resignation. Only an immeasurable, profound sadness.

They both wore the same expression they had adopted the first time they had been sitting in her office. A helpless, sorrowful countenance that even now was more striking on the huge man than on his daughter.

Kristine Håverstad still held the knife in her hand. Her father was clutching the pistol.

"Put down your weapons," she requested, almost kindly. "There!"

She was pointing at a glass table by the window. Then she and her colleague Salomonsen set to work on an entirely futile resuscitation procedure.

THURSDAY, JUNE 10

The calendar had settled down again. At long last. Low-lying cloud cover, appropriate for the time of year, was drifting across the Oslo sky, and the temperature was around fifteen degrees Celsius, the average for June. Everything was as it should be, and the citizens took relief in the knowledge that the storm damage had not been as severe as had been feared the previous day.

Hanne Wilhelmsen sat in the canteen at the police station in Grønland. Paler than everyone else, she felt sick. She had missed two nights' sleep in four days. She would go home soon. The superintendent had ordered her to stay away over the weekend. At least. Furthermore, he had asked her to apply for the post of chief inspector, something she definitely would not do. In any case and under whatever circumstances, not today. She wanted to go home.

Håkon Sand, on the other hand, appeared

unusually pleased with himself. He was sitting smiling, lost in thought, but snapped out of it when he realized that Hanne Wilhelmsen was genuinely closer to physical breakdown than he had ever seen her before.

The canteen was situated on the sixth floor, with a fantastic view. Far out on the Oslo Fjord, a Danish ship was slowly approaching land, fully laden with pensioners and luggage illegally crammed with Danish sausages and cheap bacon. The grass outside the curved building was no longer strewn with people, and only one or two optimists were stretched out, peering expectantly up at the sky to check whether the sun might return anytime soon.

"There had to be a first time," Hanne Wilhelmsen said, rubbing her eyes. "The way we let people down, it was really only a matter of time before some people took matters into their own hands. The bloody worst of it is . . ."

She restrained herself, shaking her head.

"The bloody worst of it is I understand them."

Håkon Sand scrutinized her more closely. Her hair was unwashed. Her eyes were still blue, but the black ring around the irises seemed larger, as though it had eaten its way toward the pupils. Her face seemed puffy, and her bottom lip had cracked in the middle, where a narrow, hardened line of blood divided her mouth in two.

Squinting at the bright June sunlight, her eyes followed the Danish ferry. She had not received answers to so many questions. If only she had reached the house in Bærum a few minutes earlier. Five minutes. Max.

"For instance, where did he get all that blood from?"

Uninterested, Håkon Sand shrugged his shoulders.

"I'm preoccupied with something entirely different." He brushed her question aside, gazing at her with a sly and expectant expression, in the hope that the detective inspector would ask what he was talking about.

Hanne Wilhelmsen, however, was deep in her own thoughts, and now the Danish boat was experiencing minor problems with a little cargo vessel insisting on right of way in the shipping lane. To be honest, she had not heard what he said.

"They'll probably get away with it," he said, a fraction too loudly, with a touch of bitterness at the detective inspector's lack of interest. "It's likely we won't be able to bring a prosecution against either of them!"

That helped. Letting the Danish ferry shift

336

for itself, Hanne stared at him, her eyes brimming with skepticism.

"What did you say? Get away with it?"

Kristine Håverstad and her father were being detained in custody. They had killed a man. Neither had tried to lie their way out of it. They were insistent. What's more, they had been caught in flagrante only five minutes later.

Of course they couldn't get away with it. Hanne yawned.

Håkon Sand, who had slept soundly for eight hours in his own bed, and therefore had both time and energy to study the case, and moreover had discussed it with several colleagues in the early hours of the morning, was in top form.

"Each of them claims they did it on their own," he said, taking a swig of the bitter canteen coffee. "Both of them take the blame. Each of them on their own. They obstinately deny they were operating together. From what we know at the moment, there are many aspects indicating that this at least was true. They came in their own cars and parked in different places. In addition, Kristine had made an attempt at constructing an alibi."

He smiled at the thought of the young lad who had been brought in for interrogation in a state Håkon hoped never to experience for himself. The student had thrown up twice in the first half hour of the interview.

"But that's surely not a problem, Håkon! There can't be any doubt that one of them did it, and the other must be able to be arrested as an accomplice?"

"No, actually not. Both have stories that are consistent with the facts we have. Each of them claims they killed the man and that the other one arrived immediately afterward. According to their preliminary statements, both sets of fingerprints will be on both the knife and the gun. Both have motive, both had opportunity. Both have gunshot residue on their right hands. Who shot into the ceiling and who shot the man in the arm, the parties are totally at odds about. And so, my dear chief inspector-to-be . . ."

He grinned, and she could not summon up the energy to put him right.

"And so we have quite a classic problem. In order to be found guilty, there must be proof beyond all reasonable doubt that the perpetrator committed the crime. Fifty percent is not enough! Ingenious!"

Flinging his arms out wide, he roared with laughter. People looked at them, something he realized immediately without being bothered in the slightest. Instead he got to

338

his feet and pushed the chair toward the table. He remained standing there, leaning toward the table, his hands resting on the back of the seat.

"It's too early to draw any substantial conclusions. There are many inquiries still to be undertaken. But if I'm not mistaken, the bronze lady on my desk will be splitting her sides with laughter!"

The police attorney smiled himself, from ear to ear.

"One more thing."

Now he directed his gaze in embarrassment at the tabletop, and Hanne could discern a touch of pink on his face.

"Our appointment for dinner tomorrow . . ."

She had forgotten it completely.

"Unfortunately, I'll have to cancel."

This day was proving to be full of pleasant surprises.

"That's okay," she said, conspicuously fast. "We can take a rain check."

He nodded but made no move to leave.

"I'm going to be a dad," he said eventually, and now he was truly pink around the ears. "I'm going to be a dad at Christmas! Karen and I are going to celebrate at the weekend. We're going away. I'm sorry to —"

"No problem, Håkon! Hundred percent

okay! Congratulations!"

Putting her arms around him, she hugged him for a long time.

What a day.

When she arrived back in her own office, she lifted the telephone receiver without hesitation. Before she had a chance to reconsider, she dialed an internal number.

"Are you busy tomorrow, Billy T.?"

"I've got my boys this weekend. I'm collecting them around five o'clock. Why are you asking?"

"Would you bring them with you and come for dinner at my place and . . ."

All things in moderation. She could not bring herself to say her name. He saved her.

"They are three, three, four, and five years old," he warned.

"That doesn't matter. Come at six o'clock."

Then she phoned Cecilie at work to give notice that the menu would have to be changed. It would have to be spaghetti. With loads of bright yellow fizzy drinks.

The emotion she felt as she replaced the receiver shocked her more deeply than everything that had happened during the last twenty-four dramatic hours.

She was happy!

ABOUT THE AUTHOR

Anne Holt, acclaimed author of the Hanne Wilhelmsen mysteries, has worked as a journalist and news anchor and spent two years working for the Oslo Police Department before founding her own law firm and serving as Norway's minister of justice in 1996 and 1997. She lives in Oslo with her family.

The employees of Thorndike Press hope you have enjoyed this Large Print book. All our Thorndike, Wheeler, and Kennebec Large Print titles are designed for easy reading, and all our books are made to last. Other Thorndike Press Large Print books are available at your library, through selected bookstores, or directly from us.

For information about titles, please call:
(800) 223-1244

or visit our Web site at:
http://gale.cengage.com/thorndike

To share your comments, please write:
Publisher
Thorndike Press
10 Water St., Suite 310
Waterville, ME 04901